A CHRISTMAS CAROL

By
Patrick Barlow

Adapted from the story by
Charles Dickens

samuelfrench.co.uk

FOR AMATEUR PRODUCTION ENQUIRIES

UNITED KINGDOM AND WORLD EXCLUDING NORTH AMERICA
plays@SamuelFrench-London.co.uk
020 7255 4302/01

UNITED STATES AND CANADA
info@SamuelFrench.com
1-866-598-8449

Each title is subject to availability from Samuel French, depending upon country of performance.

The UK premiere of *A Christmas Carol* was produced by Sonia Friedman
Productions at the Noël Coward Theatre, London and first performed
on 30th November, 2015
with the following cast:

Ebenezer Scrooge	**Jim Broadbent**
Bob Cratchit, Marley, Young Scrooge	**Adeel Akhtar**
Hermione Bentham, Ghost of Christmas Past, Constance, Mrs Cratchit, Mother	**Amelia Bullmore**
Frederick, Mr Grimes, Mr Fezziwig, George, Ghost of Christmas Yet to Come	**Keir Charles**
Mrs Lack, Lavinia Bentham, Mrs Grimes, Fran, Isabella, Ghost of Christmas Present, Maid	**Samantha Spiro**
Ensemble Puppeteer	**Jack Parker**
Ensemble Puppeteer	**Kim Scopes**

Director	**Phelim McDermott**
Designer	**Tom Pye**
Director of Movement	**Toby Sedgwick**
Lighting Designer	**Peter Mumford**
Sound Designer	**Gareth Fry**
Music Supervisor & Arranger	**Steven Edis**

MUSIC USE NOTE

USE OF COPYRIGHT MUSIC

IMPORTANT BILLING AND CREDIT REQUIREMENTS

This play is written for five actors and two puppeteers. Three men and three women. One actor plays Scrooge throughout. Everybody else plays everybody else.

SETTING

London

TIME

1842 and before and beyond

CHARACTERS

ACTOR ONE (M)
EBENEZER SCROOGE – standard English – 50–60

ACTOR TWO (M)
BOB CRATCHIT – cockney – 40
MARLEY'S GHOST – standard English – 50–60
YOUNG SCROOGE – standard – 16–19
LITTLE SCROOGE – standard – 8
PETER CRATCHIT – cockney – 14
KATIE CRATCHIT – cockney – 9
BOY IN STREET – cockney – 12
FREDERICK'S CHILDREN – standard – 3–12
VARIOUS NARRATORS, CAROL SINGERS, DEBTORS, SPIRITS, SKATERS,
ETC.

ACTOR THREE (F)
MRS LACK – cockney – 40
LAVINIA BENTHAM – standard – 35
MRS GRIMES – Northern English – 60
FRAN – standard – 18
ISABELLA – Sweet spoken Irish – 18–28
GHOST OF CHRISTMAS PRESENT – cockney/various 60
MARTHA CRATCHIT – cockney – 16
FREDERICK'S HOUSEMAID – cockney – 30
VARIOUS NARRATORS, CAROL SINGERS, DEBTORS, SPIRITS, SKATERS,
ETC.

ACTOR FOUR (F)
HERMIONE BENTHAM – standard – 35
GHOST OF CHRISTMAS PAST – standard – 40
CONSTANCE – standard – 30
MRS CRATCHIT – cockney – 40
MOTHER – standard – 40
VARIOUS NARRATORS, CAROL SINGERS, DEBTORS, SPIRITS, SKATERS,
ETC.

1

ACTOR FIVE (M)

FREDERICK – standard – 35

MR GRIMES – Northern English – 60

MR FEZZIWIG – Irish – 50

GEORGE – standard – 30

KATE CRATCHIT – cockney – 10

ABIGAIL CRATCHIT – cockney – 10

GHOST OF CHRISTMAS YET TO COME – standard – 50–150

PASSER–BY – cockney – 20

VARIOUS NARRATORS, CAROL SINGERS, DEBTORS, SPIRITS, SKATERS, ETC.

PUPPETEER ONE (F)

LITTLE SCROOGE, TINY TIM, VARIOUS CHILDREN, SPIRITS, PHANTOMS, URSULA CRATCHIT ETC.

PUPPETEER TWO (M)

LITTLE SCROOGE, TINY TIM, VARIOUS CHILDREN, SPIRITS, PHANTOMS, PETER CRATCHIT ETC.

ACT ONE

Prologue

FOUR ACTORS *stroll on. They are dressed in Victorian hats, coats and mufflers. There is a large door centre stage. They all stand round the door and launch into:*

CAROL: HERE WE COME A'WASSAILING.

They stop singing. They wait. No-one comes. They wait. They knock. Still no-one comes. They wait. Look at one another. Turn to the audience. They begin the tale.

ACTOR 3 Marley was dead to begin with.

ACTOR 2 Dead as a doornail.

ACTOR 4 And you can't get much deader than that.

ACTOR 5 Jacob Marley.

ACTOR 3 Dead and buried in Cripplegate graveyard.

ACTOR 4 The day before Christmas.

ACTOR 2 A year ago to the day.

ACTOR 5 Witnessed by four attendants.

ACTOR 3 The clergyman.

ACTOR 4 The clerk.

ACTOR 2 The undertaker.

ACTOR 5 And the chief and sole mourner.

ACTOR 3 Ebenezer.

ACTOR 4 Obadiah

ALL Scrooge.

3

ACTOR 2 And that was the end of it.

ACTOR 5 Or was it?

SCROOGE'S VOICE *(o.s.)* Cratchit?

> **ACTOR 2** *freezes. Immediately becomes* **CRATCHIT**.

CRATCHIT Yes sir Mr Scrooge sir?

> *The other* **ACTORS** *run off. They return with* **CRATCHIT**'s *hat, coat and scarf. They put them on him. Carry on a phonograpgh and grandfather clock. They run off, leaving* **CRATCHIT** *alone.*

> *Reveal:*

Scrooge's Counting House. Christmas Eve.
Dawn – Night

SCROOGE *stands in his counting house. Elegantly dressed in suit, cloak, bright waistcoat and top hat. Beaming brightly, he stands in a pose.*

SCROOGE Mr Cratchit!!!

CRATCHIT *snaps to attention.*

CRATCHIT Yessir Mr Scrooge sir.

SCROOGE Everything tickety-boo Mr Cratchit?

CRATCHIT Yes sir yes sir, everything tickety boo sir.

SCROOGE Splendid splendid splendid! So what are we tickety boo for *precisely* Mr Cratchit?

This is an old routine. Played out at Christmas time. CRATCHIT *has to pretend he has forgotten.*

CRATCHIT Oh! Erm – what are we – er – tickety –

SCROOGE On this particular morning?

CRATCHIT On this er – particular er –

(scratches his head) Um – er –

SCROOGE *(sings)* 'Oh come let us adore mmm! Oh mmm mmm mmm mmm mmmmm mmm!'

CRATCHIT *(as if just getting it)* Oh yes! I know! Um – wait a minute!

SCROOGE Mmm mmm mmm mmm mmmm mm –

CRATCHIT Oh yes! Er – right – er –

SCROOGE Don't over-egg it Cratchit.

CRATCHIT Right sir. Sorry sir. Um –

SCROOGE Yes?

CRATCHIT *(tentatively)* Christmas Eve sir!

SCROOGE Sorry Cratchit? Didn't quite – catch it Cratchit?

They both laugh at **SCROOGE***'s verbal dexterity.*

CRATCHIT Christmas Eve sir!

SCROOGE CHRISTMAS EVE SIR!! Well remembered Mr. Cratchit! So – ready for our little diver-tis-ment?

CRATCHIT Oooo yes sir, yes sir. Ready for our div...er...tis...ismas

CRATCHIT *looks excited.* **SCROOGE** *grabs a cord.*

SCROOGE No peeking!

CRATCHIT *closes his eyes tight.* **SCROOGE** *pulls the cord. A garland drops down. It says 'A PROSPEROUS CHRISTMAS EVE TO OUR ALL ESTEEMED CUSTOMERS'.*

And open!

CRATCHIT *opens his eyes. He sees the garland. He applauds.*

(bows extravagantly) Thank you thank you thank you. Most kind! Most kind!

CRATCHIT I must say I do enjoy our little um –

SCROOGE Yes that's enough Cratchit.

CRATCHIT Sorry sir.

Door bell goes. They both jump. The pupetteers have sprung into action and have bought the door on – from now on they control the door as it comes on and off.

SCROOGE Ah! First customer Cratchit?

CRATCHIT *runs to desk, looks at a unwieldy ledger.*

CRATCHIT That's right sir. First customer sir. Six o'clock sir.

CRATCHIT *runs to the door.*

SCROOGE Clock Cratchit!

CRATCHIT *runs to the clock. Winds it to ten past six.*

CRATCHIT!!!

CRATCHIT *runs to phonograph. Clicks switch.*

MUSIC (PHONOGRAPH): WE WISH YOU A MERRY CHRISTMAS.

Enter!!!

CRATCHIT *runs to the door. Out of breath now. Opens it. Reveals* MRS LACK. *Shivering with cold and nerves. She throws snow over her head.*

CRATCHIT Mrs Lack sir.

SCROOGE Sorry?

CRATCHIT Mrs er Lack sir.

SCROOGE Mrs –

(takes this in) – Lack. My dear lady! Doo come in won't you please!

MRS LACK Thank you sir, thank you.

CRATCHIT *shuts door behind her.* MRS LACK *enters.*

SCROOGE Charming charming. *Charmant* as the French would say. Do sit down Mrs Lack. Take the lovely lovely comfy seat why don't you? Cratchit!

CRATCHIT *brings a chair.*

Sit Mrs Lack!

MRS LACK *sits. The chair is quite low.*

A little late Mrs Lack.

MRS LACK *(looks at clock, surprised)* Oh! I was sure it was –

SCROOGE Well we'll let it go this time but *do* try and keep your appointments Mrs Lack. Don't want any 'bad feeling' between us do we?

MRS LACK No sir. Right sir.

SCROOGE So where were we? Ah yes!

(beams) Carry on dear lady.

MRS LACK Well – um I was wondrin' might I'n bein' addressin' Mr Marley sir.

SCROOGE *(gasps with grief)* Mr Marley! Sadly no. Mr Marley is... no longer with us.

MRS LACK Erm –

SCROOGE He sings with the choir invisible.

MRS LACK Er –

SCROOGE He hath shuffled off this mortal coil.

MRS LACK Shuffled his what sir?

SCROOGE His final thread is spun.

MRS LACK Fred?

SCROOGE Thread Madam! He is dead!

MRS LACK Oh dear oh dear! I'm so sorry sir!

SCROOGE But a single year ago. To the day in fact. Nearly to the very hour.

(bigger sob) Such a dear dear dear friend.

CRATCHIT *brings a box of Victorian tissues to* SCROOGE. SCROOGE *blows his nose loudly. Hands used tissue back to* CRATCHIT. CRATCHIT *folds it neatly and puts delicately back into the box.*

But the faceless executioner, the great leveller himself, comes to us all in his time, doth he not dear lady?

(bows deeply) Ebenezer Scrooge. At your service.

MRS LACK *(stands, curtsies)* Most honoured sir thankin' you sir.

SCROOGE Sit Mrs Lack.

MRS LACK *sits.*

So my dear lady, how may we assist?

MRS LACK Well sir – it's like this sir –

SCROOGE Take your time.

MRS LACK Thank you, thank you sir.

(takes breath) It's my husband sir you see sir. He's a good man sir, honest man sir. It's just – well there's no work sir and what with seven kiddies –

SCROOGE Seven what – sorry?

MRS LACK Kiddies sir!

SCROOGE Kiddies! Ah!

(chuckles knowingly) Bit of a handful eh?

MRS LACK Oh yes sir yes. And no food on the table sir and – what with it bein' Christmas sir and –

SCROOGE Did you say – Christmas?

MRS LACK Erm –

A signal to **CRATCHIT**. **CRATCHIT** *sets off phonograph.*

MUSIC (PHONOGRAPH): IT CAME UPON A MIDNIGHT CLEAR.

MRS LACK *looks enchanted.*

SCROOGE A blessed time is it not Mrs Lack?

MRS LACK Oh yes indeed sir.

SCROOGE Yet costly too methinks!

MRS LACK Oh yes indeed indeed it is sir.

SCROOGE Indeed indeedy Mrs Lack.

He laughs merrily. **MRS LACK** *laughs,* **CRATCHIT** *laughs.*

So – might I suggest a little advance might not go amiss?

MRS LACK *(not sure what he means)* Sorry sir? Um – advance – er –

SCROOGE Lolly Mrs Lack!

MRS LACK Lolly? – erm –

SCROOGE Boodle –

MRS LACK Er –

He comes very close.

SCROOGE *MONEY my dear sweet lady!?*

MUSIC (PHONOGRAPH): WINDS DOWN.

MRS LACK I wasn't wishin' to presume sir!

(she stands and curtsies) But yes sir! Indeed sir!

SCROOGE Sit Mrs Lack!

MRS LACK *sits.*

MRS LACK Thank you thank you kindly sir!

SCROOGE Tis nothing madam. Tis the duty of our trade after all. Us financiers. To help all those in need.Tis our sacred purpose, is it not Mr Cratchit? So you see my dear lady you've come to the perfect person for your predicament. And with any luck Mrs Lack you won't be Mrs 'lack' any more! And all your little 'kiddies' will have full little tummies.

He laughs merrily. **CRATCHIT** *laughs merrily.*

MRS LACK Oh sir! Oh sir!!

SCROOGE Mr Cratchit if you please. Follow us madam.

SCROOGE *and* **MRS LACK** *follow* **CRATCHIT** *into the Deposit room. Full of drawers and boxes. In the middle of the room is an enormous chest.* **SCROOGE** *takes a large jangling chain of keys from his waistcoat pocket. Finds the right key. Hands it to* **CRATCHIT.** **CRATCHIT** *reaches for it.*

Don't snatch it Cratchit!

He laughs merrily. They all laugh merrily.

CRATCHIT Sorry sir.

SCROOGE *gives him the key.* **CRATCHIT** *uses it to unlock another drawer which produces another key and so on – until finally the right key is revealed.* **SCROOGE** *uses this key to unlock the padlock.* **SCROOGE** *throws back the lid. A golden light shines out of the box.*

MUSIC: BARBASTELLA - 'BATMAN BEGINS' SOUNDTRACK.

MRS LACK *and* **CRATCHIT** *peer in and gasp.* **MRS LACK** *nearly faints at the sight.*

MRS LACK Oh my oh my sir!

SCROOGE So what shall we say Mrs Lack?

(takes out a pound) A pound?

MRS LACK *(gasping with amazement)* A pound! A pound would be just – oh sir –

SCROOGE *(holds up two pounds)* Or – two pounds?

MRS LACK *(overwhelmed)* Two!

SCROOGE Or – perhaps –

(he holds up the five pounds) – five pounds?

MRS LACK *(swooning)* FIVE!!! FIVE POUNDS SIR!!! Oh my! Oh my! Thank you sir thank you!

He proffers the coins to **MRS LACK** *who reaches eagerly for them. At the last moment, he clamps them in his fist.*

SCROOGE At what shall we say? One hundred percent?

MRS LACK *(bewildered)* One hun – um –

SCROOGE Forgive me, I'm sorry. Did I not make myself quite clear? I am referring to the interest madam.

MRS LACK Erm – sorry, inter – em sorry?

SCROOGE The IN-TER-EST Mrs Lack! I can hardly lend you five pounds for nothing. Can I Mr Cratchit?

CRATCHIT No sir no sir!

SCROOGE No no no sir!

(draws closer to **MRS LACK***)* All it is is this. It's really very simple. I lend you five shiny pounds from my big black box. You have all your lovely Christmas treats for all your little kiddies!

You give me back – how much would Mrs Lack give me back Cratchit? CRATCHIT!!

CRATCHIT Five pounds sir.

SCROOGE Five pounds sir.

MRS LACK *(anxious)* Five pounds sir?

SCROOGE Exactement madame! Which on top of the five I loaned you comes to – er –

CRATCHIT Ten pounds.

SCROOGE In toto. Which you pay me –

(thinks about it) – in a week.

MRS LACK In a wee – Ten pounds!?? But HOW? WHEN!!?? How could I POSSIBLY –

SCROOGE Oh well I shouldn't really, I'm too generous, I'm a fool to myself – but seeing as it's Christmas – let's say – three months?

MRS LACK Three months! Oh thank you sir!

(kissing his hand) Thank you thank you thank you sir –

SCROOGE And the interest on that Mr Cratchit – give or take a penny or two – would be –

CRATCHIT Seventy-five pounds sir.

SCROOGE Speak up Cratchit!

CRATCHIT Seventy-five pounds sir!

SCROOGE *(loudly)* Seventy-five pounds sir!

MRS LACK *(gasping)* Seventy – five – in a – in a – in three – But I could never ever – Oh Mr Scrooge sir! Have a heart sir! I beg of 'ee sir!

SCROOGE Have a heart!!?? Have a HEART!!!??? Have a heart for those poor little starving kiddies Mrs Lack!!! Do you actually care Mrs Lack!? WHAT KIND OF MOTHER ARE YOU!!!!???

MRS LACK *looks racked.* **CRATCHIT** *looks racked.* **SCROOGE** *turns away.*

Oh well! Tried to help!

About to drop coins back in the box.

MRS LACK No no no no no sir!!! Please sir please sir please sir please sir!

SCROOGE *turns, magnanimously beaming.*

SCROOGE Splendid. *Splendide.* The three month option then? Excellent. So just a little tiny little signature if you'd be so kind. Thank you Mr Cratchit? QUICKLY!!

They all walk back into the front of the shop. **SCROOGE** *pushes* **MRS LACK** *back in her seat.* **CRATCHIT** *runs over with papers and quill.*

Just here please?

(**MRS LACK** *scribbles,* **CRATCHIT** *reveals another paper*) And er – just here.

(she scribbles, another) And another little one.

(she scribbles) Thank you. And – er – here.

(she scribbles) And oh! One more just here.

(she scribbles faster) And – sorry! – another just here.

(even faster) And one more. Initial!

(even faster) Initial!

(faster) Full signature!

(faster) Initial!

(faster) Initial!

(faster) Initial!

(faster) Initial!

(faster) Full signature!

(faster) Full!

(faster) Initial!

(faster) Full!

(faster) Initial!

(faster) Full!

(faster) Initial!

(faster) Full!

(faster) Initial!

(faster) And another full signature there.

(faster) And the last one!

(faster) And one more. *Quickly!* And one more!

(scribbles last signature) Thank you!!! Thank you Cratchit.

CRATCHIT *whisks away the papers.* **SCROOGE** *holds the coins up.*

So Mrs Lack! Five lovely jubbly poundies. To you madam.

He drops them one at a time into her palm.

There. That wasn't too painful was it?

The door appears. **SCROOGE** *opens the door for* **MRS LACK** *and shoves her out.*

Good day to you Mrs. Lack.

MRS LACK *throws snow over her head. Exits hurriedly. The door retreats. The door returns.*

The shop door-bell clangs.

FREDERICK, SCROOGE's *nephew, enters. He throws snow over himself.*

Quick quick quick! Another customer! Hurry Cratchit! Cratchit! Cratchit! Cratchit! Cratchit!

CRATCHIT *runs to the phonograph. Turns it back on.*

SCROOGE *preens. Turns back beaming.*

Doooo come in why don't you? And to whom do I have the –

CRATCHIT It is not a new customer sir! It is your nephew Frederick!

SCROOGE *freezes.*

SCROOGE I know who it is Cratchit!

FREDERICK My dear uncle Scrooge!

SCROOGE My dear nephew Frederick. And what can I do for you sir?

FREDERICK You know what you can do for me sir!

(gives CRATCHIT *his hat)* Thank you Mr Cratchit. You can accept my invitation to Christmas dinner sir. Which I most heartily invite you to every year sir. To share Christmas Day with myself, my wife Constance, and my family sir.

SCROOGE And the reply sir is the same as it is every year sir. No sir. Thank ye for the invitation sir. I have no wish to share Christmas with anyone. Least of all yourself or your – *wretched family sir!* Good day to thee sir!

(turns away. Turns back) Have you not left sir?

FREDERICK But why sir?

SCROOGE Why what sir?

FREDERICK Will you not come sir?

SCROOGE Because dear nephew – as I inform you every tedious year sir – I veritably, utterly and indubitably HATE CHRISTMAS!!!

FREDERICK So what is all this uncle?

(indicates banner) – and this uncle?

(indicates phonogram) A Christmas carol unless I am mistaken! Christmas cheer is it not!

He winds up the phonograph.

MUSIC (PHONOGRAPH): WE WISH YOU A MERRY CHRISTMAS.

SCROOGE *snaps off the phonograph.*

MUSIC (PHONOGRAPH): CUT.

SCROOGE Nothing of the sort sir, I'm sorry to disappoint you! This sir is the latest 'thing' in business if you wish to know sir and that is all it is. 'Tis remarkably efficacious in separating credulous fools from their money and maximising profits. What do we call it Cratchit?

CRATCHIT 'Marketing' sir.

SCROOGE 'Marketing' sir. Not half clever eh? One day it will rule the world.

SCROOGE *chuckles.* CRATCHIT *chuckles uneasily.*

But on no account allow its dreadful jollity to deceive you dear nephew. Tis all tinsel falsity, and means nothing sir. Like Christmas itself sir! Which you are welcome to! Good morrow sir and good riddance. Hat Cratchit! Door Cratchit!

CRATCHIT Yes sir!

CRATCHIT *collects* FREDERICK's *hat, summons the door. The door returns.* CRATCHIT *opens it. He waits, shivering, holding out* FREDERICK's *hat.* FREDERICK *marches to the door. Instead of leaving, he closes the door. The door retreats.*

SCROOGE I said DOOR Cratchit!

CRATCHIT Yes sir!

CRATCHIT *summons the door. The door returns.* CRATCHIT *holds out* FREDERICK's *hat. Shivers at the door.* FREDERICK *does not move. Sends the door away.*

FREDERICK Sorry Mr Cratchit.

The door retreats.

SCROOGE Did ye not hear me Cratchit!?

CRATCHIT *summons the door. The door returns.*

CRATCHIT (*to* FREDERICK) Sorry sir.

FREDERICK *sends the door away. The door retreats.*

FREDERICK *(to* CRATCHIT*)* Sorry sir.

SCROOGE I said did ye not hear me Cratchit!!

CRATCHIT *freezes in terror. Caught between the two.*

FREDERICK And will ye not hear *ME* sir! A Christmas feast uncle! A roaring fire sir! A fine plump turkey sir! Chestnut stuffing! Roast potatoes! Cranberry sauce, brussel sprouts and gravy sir!

CRATCHIT *listens yearningly.*

CRATCHIT Graaaaavy!!!

SCROOGE Gruel sir!!!!

FREDERICK No sir no! A true Christmas table uncle! All alight with smiling faces! Joy on every countenance! Music and dancing and –

SCROOGE – and pathetic paltry parlour games I should imagine sir!!!

FREDERICK Yes uncle yes! All manner of games sir! O uncle dearest uncle!! What *IS* it about Christmas uncle makes you so unhappy!?

SCROOGE Christmas sir is a fraud sir! A sham sir! A fake sir! Just like this – paper *chain* sir!

(he rips down the banner) What is the excellently expressive and – if I may say so – hilarious word I use for 'Christmas' Cratchit? Cratchit!!

CRATCHIT *(inaudible)* Humbug sir.

SCROOGE Louder sir!

CRATCHIT *(a little louder)* Humbug sir.

SCROOGE Louder!

CRATCHIT Humbug sir!!

SCROOGE LOUDER!!

CRATCHIT HUMBUG SIR!!!

SCROOGE HUMBUG SIR!!!

FREDERICK No sir! Not Humbug sir!! Tis the opposite sir! Tis an honest time sir! A merry time sir! Full of cheer and goodness! When all the world is good and glad sir!

SCROOGE Cheer! Glad! Good! Honest! Merry! Yukkkkk! If I could work my will nephew, every buffoon who wastes his hours of righteous toil spreading Christmas cheer to all and sundry, would be boiled with his own Christmas pudding and buried in his grave with a stake of Christmas holly through his heart!

FREDERICK I cannot believe uncle – that *somewhere* inside you, resides not a memory – a tiny spark of light glowing in your heart – when Christmas was a goodly time to you too sir! When you could say with an open heart, with all the world, God bless it everyone!

CRATCHIT *(applauds)* God bless it every one sir!

SCROOGE CRATCHIT!

> **CRATCHIT** *freezes.*

One more sound from you Cratchit and you'll keep your Christmas by losing your blessed situation sir! I can snuff you out Cratchit. Like a candle Cratchit. Or a moth Cratchit. Just like –

(clicks fingers) – that Cratchit!

CRATCHIT Yes Sir.

FREDERICK Dear uncle –

SCROOGE WHAT!!!?

FREDERICK Come for my mother then!

> **SCROOGE** *starts.*

For thy dear sister's sake! For Fran.

SCROOGE My sister sir!!!? My sister is gone sir! Long gone and forgotten sir! I think thine ears are sealed sir!! Nothing will induce me to come, sir! NOTHING!!!

FREDERICK But my wife sir! My darling Constance! My children! They long to meet you sir!

SCROOGE No-one longs to meet me sir! NOW BE GONE SIR!!!

FREDERICK This shell that entombs thee uncle! Like a dark cave sir! Why sir – why – why –

SCROOGE WHY DID YOU GET MARRIED SIR?

All freeze. CRATCHIT *freezes.* SCROOGE *freezes.*

FREDERICK What?

SCROOGE What?

FREDERICK Why did I get –

SCROOGE Nothing sir!

FREDERICK Because I fell in love.

SCROOGE Love!? Ha! LOVE!!??

The shop door bell clangs.

All freeze. CRATCHIT *rushes to the oncoming door. Opens it to see who it is – then promptly closes it – much to the* BENTHAM's *dismay.*

CRATCHIT Two ladies sir!

SCROOGE Ladies!!? *Ladies!!?* Quickly Cratchit quickly!

CRATCHIT *winds the phonograph.* SCROOGE *plumps his tie, flounces his hair, smooths his eyebrows.*

MUSIC (PHONOGRAPH): JOY TO THE WORLD.

FREDERICK *stands there, as they run round him.* CRATCHIT *finally opens the door. Reveal* LAVINIA *and* HERMIONE BENTHAM. *They throw snow over their heads.* SCROOGE *switches on his instant smile.*

My dear ladies! Doooo come in if you would please!

The ladies enter. CRATCHIT *shuts the door. Sends it away.*

LAVINIA & HERMIONE Thank you sir most kindly sir.

SCROOGE Coats Cratchit!

CRATCHIT, *still clutching his book, takes their coats.*

LAVINIA *(to* FREDERICK*)* And to whom do we have the honour Mr Marley or Mr Scrooge sir?

SCROOGE *(steps in front of* FREDERICK, *bows)* Ebenezer Scrooge at your service ladies. Mr Marley sadly...

(stifled sob) ...is no longer...

(bigger sob) ...forgive me...

(giant sob) ...a year ago to the day...

CRATCHIT *passes the tissue.* SCROOGE *prepares to take it.*

HERMIONE BENTHAM My dear dear dear Mr Scrooge sir!

SCROOGE *switches off his sad face puts on his bright face and* CRATCHIT *puts away the tissue.*

SCROOGE So anyway ladies or – as the French would say – *mesdames*, let us –

(he brightens) – cut to the chase shall we?

LAVINIA The – er – chase?

SCROOGE A little Christmas loan perhaps? Cratchit!

CRATCHIT *picks up loan papers and quill. Also juggles the appointments diary and the coats. Re-winds the phonograph.*

HERMIONE A loan?

SCROOGE Or –

(beaming) – two possibly? Two little Christmas loans perhaps?

HERMIONE No no no sir. You mistake our purpose. We come for your charity sir.

MUSIC (PHONOGRAPH): WINDS DOWN.

SCROOGE *stops beaming.*

SCROOGE My what?

LAVINIA For the poor, the needy, the destitute, all who suffer at this Christmas tide.

SCROOGE Are there no prisons?

HERMIONE Prisons?

SCROOGE Or workhouses? Are the Treadmill and the Poor Law not in full vigour?

HERMIONE They are indeed sir. I wish I could say they were not.

LAVINIA So – what may we put you down for?

SCROOGE Down for?

FREDERICK Down for uncle?

(takes out some coins) Here madam. Tis not much. But it is something.

LAVINIA AND HERMIONE Oh! Thank you sir, thank you kindly sir! Most generous sir!

They all turn to **SCROOGE.**

HERMIONE Sir?

SCROOGE *looks at them.*

SCROOGE Nothing.

HERMIONE Ah! You wish to be anonymous.

(to Lavinia) He wishes to be anonymous.

SCROOGE I wish to do my business madam. I help support the prisons and the workhouses if you care to know. And those who are 'poor and destitute' as you call them must simply go there and be quiet about it. And if they are too WEAK to go there madam, then they had better die without delay. And decrease the surplus population. Do us all a favour. Sorry ladies but this is the way the world is made. Boo hoo hoo but there we are. Good night ladies!

The **BENTHAMS** *stand frozen.*

I said GOOD NIGHT LADIES!

He bows. The **BENTHAMS** *hastily grab their coats from* **CRATCHIT**. *There is a jumble of coats as* **CRATCHIT** *summons the door. The door returns.* **CRATCHIT** *opens the door for them. The* **BENTHAMS** *tumble out and exit.* **CRATCHIT** *runs after them, throws snow after them. Returns to the Counting House.* **CRATCHIT** *shuts the door.* **CRATCHIT** *sends the door away.* **FREDERICK** *turns to* **SCROOGE.**

FREDERICK I am very sorry for thee uncle.

SCROOGE Keep your sorrow for yourself sir!

FREDERICK If you could listen to your own heart dear uncle –

SCROOGE My heart sir? My heart ceased to beat many years ago sir. Cratchit!

    CRATCHIT *summons the door.*

FREDERICK Thank you Mr Cratchit.

CRATCHIT Thank you sir.

    FREDERICK *exits.* **CRATCHIT** *waits.* **FREDERICK** *returns.* **CRATCHIT** *takes his hat and this time he exits through the door.* **CRATCHIT** *realises his mistake and walks around the door to enter the Counting House. Hands* **FREDERICK** *his hat back.*

FREDERICK Thank you Mr Cratchit.

CRATCHIT Thank you sir.

    FREDERICK *exits.* **CRATCHIT** *throws snow over him. Shuts the door. Sends the door away.*

    CRATCHIT *back to his desk.*

    SCROOGE *stands stock still, brooding in the gathering darkness.*

MUSIC: SHOSTAKOVICH 8TH SYMPHONY - 4TH MOVEMENT. 0-14.

CRATCHIT *tentatively puts on his cap and muffler. He plucks up courage, creeps up behind* SCROOGE.

MUSIC: FADES.

Sir?

SCROOGE *does not move.*

If it's – quite convenient sir –

SCROOGE Convenient sir? Convenient for what sir!?

CRATCHIT To bid you goodnight sir.

SCROOGE Goodnight sir!? GOODNIGHT SIR!!? No it's not convenient sir. Not convenient one jot sir!

CRATCHIT But sir it's – closing time sir.

SCROOGE Closing time! Closing time! It's always *closing time* isn't it! Go on then Cratchit! Away with ye! Back first thing tomorrow!

CRATCHIT Tomorrow sir!? But it's Christmas Day tomorrow sir!

SCROOGE So?

CRATCHIT Only day we're all together sir. The family sir. Tiny Tim's been looking forward to it all year sir.

SCROOGE Tiny what!?

CRATCHIT Tim sir.

SCROOGE Tiny Tim!!??

CRATCHIT My littlest one sir.

SCROOGE Gorging yourselves on some profligate Christmas bean-feast no doubt!

CRATCHIT Yes sir. Sorry sir.

SCROOGE Which I shall be paying for! Picking a man's pocket every twenty-fifth of December! It's not fair sir d'ye hear me? Just not fair.

But don't think about me, no no no, don't spare a thought for others will you! Back on Boxing Day Cratchit! Before the first light cracks the sky! Or – it's the – hatchet Cratchit!

CRATCHIT *(laughs along)* Very good sir. Yes sir. And a very happy –

SCROOGE Exit Cratchit!

> **CRATCHIT** *calls for door. Door returns.* **CRATCHIT** *runs out.*

LATCHET CRATCHIT!!!

> **CRATCHIT** *slams door. Throws snow over himself.* **CRATCHIT** *exits. The door follows him.*

> **SCROOGE** *stands all alone.*

> *Street sounds. Distant shrieks and cries of children.*

Listen to 'em all! Little *kiddies!* Snowballing and tobogganing and – SKATING!

(shouts through window) I hope the ice breaks! Hope it snaps and cracks beneath the lot of yer! Hope you SKATE YOUR WAY TO HELL!

MUSIC: SUICIDE GHOST – 'SIXTH SENSE' SOUNDTRACK.

> **SCROOGE** *walks into the Deposit room – he sees his chest of money, and flings open the lid. He kneels before it. The golden light shines into his face. He thrusts his hands into the coins. They tumble through his fingers. He talks to them lovingly.*

You won't run out on me will you money? You won't desert me? We are safe together you and I. Are we not? We cannot be parted! Not ever! *(shouts up into the skies)* And you! Ha ha!! Can't get your hands on it now can you, you old devil! Cos you're dead and buried Jacob Marley! Still dead as a doornail! And you can't get much deader than that! Ha ha ha! Can you Jacob! Eh? Ha ha ha!

> *Slams down the lid and locks the padlock tight with his jangling keys.*

Ha ha ha ha! Eh? Sorry? Did you say something? Must have missed it! Ha ha ha!

> *The door gently returns. The* **ACTORS** *reappear. Sing.*

CAROL SINGERS
> LULLY, LULLAY, THOU LITTLE TINY CHILD,
> BY, BY, LULLY, LULLAY. LULLAY,
> THOU LITTLE TINY CHILD.
> BY, BY, LULLY, LULLAY.

Suddenly the door opens. There is **SCROOGE**! *He charges them, shouting.*

SCROOGE Gaaaah!!! Gaaaah!!!

The **CAROL SINGERS** *scatter and disappear screaming.*

MUSIC: PROKOVIEV – LIEUTENANT KIJE: TROIKA.

London Streets. Christmas Eve. Night

Loud London street sounds. Horses hooves, trundling coaches, barrel organ, people excited, selling wares.

ACTOR 3 And so on that Christmas Eve, Ebenezer Scrooge locked his premises and wended his way home.

ACTOR 5 Past the bright lights of shops he went.

ACTOR 4 Full and glowing with sweetmeats and holly sprigs and bright red berries.

ACTOR 2 And mince pies and plum puddings, and boiling hot chestnuts –

ACTOR 5 And sausages and suckling pigs and the greatest white feathered turkey ever seen on any Christmas Eve in the great memory of Christmases!

ACTOR 3 But Scrooge – as he made his lonely way home –

Sound effects & music stops.

– saw none of it.

MUSIC: INTRO AND FIRST VERSE: CAROL - THIS IS THE TRUTH FROM ABOVE (VAUGHAN WILLIAMS - FANTASIA ON CHRISTMAS CAROLS)

Shadow play in lighted windows. Different happy Christmases are seen as **SCROOGE** *plods past.*

Scrooge's Bedroom. Christmas Eve. Night

Lights come up. **SCROOGE** *sitting alone in bed in nightshirt and nightcap, in one hand he holds a single candle illuminating his face and in the other a meagre soup bowl. He slurps noisily from his soup bowl. The other* **ACTORS** *and* **PUPPETEERS** *are spirits in the* **SHADOWS** *or off-stage.*

SCROOGE *(mimics* **FREDERICK***)* Oooh! Christmas uncle! Visit us for Christmas uncle Scrooge! Christmas Day with Constance! Constance and the family! Oooh!! Constance Constance Constance Constance!

(slurps his soup. Mimics **HERMIONE***)* And ooooh Mr Scrooge sir! Remember the poor and the destitute! All lonely at Christmas Time!

(slurps his soup. mimics **CRATCHIT***)* And oh Mr Scrooge sir, if it's all the same with you sir? I have to go home to Mrs Cratchit sir and all the little snatchit Cratchits sir, if you're sure sir, if it's quite conveeenient sir? Well it's not sir! Not conveeenient! Not conveeeenient one bit sir!

Scraping chain sounds.

SCROOGE *looks up. Listens.*

Chain sounds stop.

Goes back to his soup. Another slurp. It tastes disgusting. He spits it back in the bowl.

Yuk!!! Plain wicked is what it is sir! D'ye hear me sir!!??

Chain sounds. Louder.

He looks up again. Looks behind him.

Chain sounds stop.

Continues slurping...

VOICE *(o.s.) (whisper)* Scrooge... Scrooge... Scrooge...

SCROOGE *stops slurping. Calls into the darkness.*

SCROOGE Hello!!? Who's that!!?

Silence. He gets out of bed, crosses the stage. Holds out the candle. Peers into the darkness.

VOICE *(o.s.) (whisper, louder)* Scrooge!

SCROOGE *stops, spins round.*

Chain sounds.

SCROOGE *freezes, wide-eyed, fast breathing.*

SCROOGE I know that voice! Can't be! Hah!!
(shouts into the shadows) Who *IS* that!? Come OUT NOW! Do you hear me!?

Chain sounds.

Whispering and laughter.

Who is it!!? Where are you!?

VOICE *(o.s.) (whisper louder)* Here Ebenezer! Ebeneeeezer! Heeeere Ebeneeeezer! Heeeere!

SCROOGE Where are you? Where?

SCROOGE *creeps towards the chains, the whispering and laughter, further and further into the shadows. He peers into the darkness with the burning candle.*

FLASH of thunder and lightning.

MARLEY'S GHOST *appears, pulling on chains.*

MUSIC: SUICIDE GHOST – 'SIXTH SENSE' SOUNDTRACK.

SCROOGE *shrieks. He rolls across the floor. Shouts into the darkness.*

Get back sir! Get back I tell thee!! Who are you sir? Who are you? Who are you sir!?

FLASH of thunder and lightning.

MARLEY TIS I EBENEZER!!! Jacob Marley!! Returned from the grave sir!!!

SCROOGE MARLEY!!?? Marley!!??? Returned from the – No no no sir! You are – ha ha ha! Not he sir! For he is – as door as a dead-nail. As dale as a door-ned. As ned as a nob-dod. And you – you are – you are –

(steadying himself) – an infection of the mind sir. Is what you are sir! Caused by a crumb of cheese, a fragment of underdone potato, an undigested piece of roast beef. Grave sir!? There is more of gravy than of grave about you sir! You are not he sir!

(he laughs loudly) Ha ha ha ha ha!!!

MARLEY Then I shall prove it to thee that I am sir. Remember mine face sir? A face like ancient parchment so it was said sir.

The **GHOST** *reveals his face. He shrieks into* **SCROOGE**'s *face.*

AGGGGGHHHHHHHHHHHHH!

SCROOGE AGGGGGHHHHHHHHHHHHH!

SCROOGE *leaps back. Staggers to his feet.*

Oh no no no no sir!!! You will not frighten me sir with all your ghosty tricks sir! I am very sorry if thou art decomposing but it is hardly my problem. Put a brave face on it sir!

(he laughs) Don't go to pieces! Pull yourself together man!

(laughs again) Geddit? You rotter! Ha ha ha!

MARLEY *(unmoved)* True. It is not your problem. Yet. But soon it will be. For you bear the same fetters as I.

SCROOGE What fetters?

MARLEY These fetters.

MARLEY *stumbles as if dragging a great weight.*

Chain sounds.

'Tis the chain I forged in life Ebenezer. And, attached to it, all the dreadful *accoutrements* of my trade! Cash boxes, padlocks, heavy keys – *OUR* trade Ebenezer! Of my own free will did I wear it. As do you sir.

SCROOGE Me sir! I have no chain sir! Ha ha! I am –

(a jaunty little twirl) – chain-free sir!

MARLEY Only at the end willst thou seest it.

SCROOGE End? End of what? What end?

MARLEY Thine end sir! That thou art eternally and irrevocably trapped! As I am!

(comes close) Shall I tell thee why?

SCROOGE I'd rather you didn't actually.

MARLEY Because, dear Ebenezer, never once did we help a single human soul without some profit attached to it!

SCROOGE So?

MARLEY SO? SO?!?? That is not why we are here sir! Upon the earth sir! That is not our sacred purpose! To gain. To profit. To make MONEY sir*!*

SCROOGE Well I happen to believe it is sir!

MARLEY NO SIR! NO EBENEZER! To help others! *That* is our sacred duty sir!

SCROOGE *listens then laughs in his face.*

SCROOGE *Humbug sir!* My sacred duty is to help myself sir! Help others!? *Ha!!!*

MARLEY *(sobbing) NOOOO NOOOO EBENEZER!!!!*

SCROOGE Listen Marley! Your fate is your fate. And my fate is mine. And I have nothing to be *SAVED* from thank you! So kindly leave me to the rest of my days. That I shall live out as I see fit. Thank you sir for your concern sir! But now –

Runs to the window, flings it open. A wild wind blows in.

Wind sounds.

– *OUT* if you would please!

(tries to waft him out) Out sir out!! Whoosh! Whoosh! Away away sir!!

MARLEY Then in that case – it is decided!

SCROOGE What? What is decided?

MARLEY Scroooge! Scrooooge!

SCROOGE WHAT!?

MARLEY Three ghosts will visit you. This very night.

SCROOGE Ghosts? Three ghosts!!?

MARLEY The first cometh at the last stroke of twelve. The second, at the third stroke of three expect. And the third at the second cock crow that doth herald forth the dawn.

SCROOGE Can you repeat that please?

MARLEY I'd rather not actually. Repent sir! Open thy heart to humanity!

SCROOGE Open my heart!!? To humanity!!?? But I hate humanity you know that!!

MARLEY Then it is too late sir. There is no stopping them sir!

SCROOGE What!!?? Damn you Marley damn you!

MARLEY I am already damned sir!

Haunting sounds of grief and regret.

MUSIC: *BATMAN BEGINS : VESPERTILIO.*

SHADOWS *or* **PUPPETS** *appear behind* **SCROOGE.**

SCROOGE What's this? Who are these? These – shadows? What are they? Marley! Marley!!

The **SHADOWS** *start to slowly fly round him.*

MARLEY The damned sir! The lost! The phantoms of all the inconsolable souls! All those who lost the chance to help their fellows in life! And now weep for ever in HELL!

SCROOGE In hell?

MARLEY In hell! Just as you will Ebenezer!

Music and weeping build.

The **SHADOWS** *fly round the auditorium.* **SCROOGE** *shudders with ill-concealed terror as he watches them.*

SHADOWS Forgive us! Forgive us! Forgive us!!

MARLEY But I think thou dost knowest them sir. Look closely sir.

MARLEY *starts to wrap his head.* **SCROOGE** *peers at the phantoms as they pass.*

SCROOGE What? Who!? Marley!!??

MARLEY Farewell Scrooge!

Finishes wrapping his head. Exits.

SCROOGE *gasps as he recognises the phantoms!*

SCROOGE Ah!!! I dost! I know these men! I dost! I mean I do!! Aghh! *(pointing as they pass)* Bankers, brokers, loan men, bailiffs!

SHADOWS Forgive us! Forgive us! Forgive us!!

SCROOGE Factory owners, mill owners, pit owners! Slave drivers!

The spirits fly faster and faster. **SCROOGE** *ducks and shrieks.*

Aggghhh!

SHADOWS Forgive us! Forgive us! Forgive us!!

SCROOGE And look! There! A load of – agggh! Politicians I see! Indeed one whole government all padlocked together.

A host of **PUPPETS** *appear as the government.*

SHADOWS Help! Help!! Forgive us! Forgive us! We said we cared for the people! But we did not care at all! And now we do, but it's too late! Too late!

MARLEY *(voice over)* Repent Scrooge! Change thine ways!

SCROOGE *(spins round)* Marley! MARLEY!!!!?

MARLEY *(voice over)* Up here Ebenezer!

SCROOGE *looks for* **MARLEY** *amongst the spirits.*

Lost Ebenezer!!! Lost foreeeeeeever!

SHADOWS Lost foreeeeeeever! Foreeeeeeever!

SCROOGE Marley!

MARLEY Repent Scrooge! Change thine ways! Don't become like me Scrooge! Don't become like US!

SHADOWS Don't become like US!!!!!!!

MARLEY Repent Scrooge! While there is still time!!

SHADOWS Time Scrooge! Repent Scrooge! Change Scrooge!! Repent! Time! Change! Time! Change! Repent! Time!

The words of the spirits fill the theatre.

The **SHADOWS** *fly faster and faster round* **SCROOGE** *and the auditorium. He stands wide-eyed with terror but refusing to yield.*

SCROOGE CHANGE!!??? REPENT!!!?? STILL TIME!!?? HUMBUG SIR!!! HA HA HA!!! NO NO NO!!! I SHALL NEVER CHANGE! D'YE HEAR ME!!?? NEVER NEVER REPENT!!

MARLEY & SHADOWS Chaaaaange Scrooooge! CHANGE!!! REPENT!!! REPENT!!! REPENNNT!!!

SCROOGE DID YE NOT HEAR ME SIR!!! NEVER SIR!!!!! Ha ha ha ha ha!!!! NEVER! NEVER NEVER NEVER! HUMBUG HUMBUG HUMBUG HUMBUUUUUUUUUUG!!!

Music Climaxes – cuts out. Blackout.

Scrooge's Bedroom – Christmas Eve. Midnight

Lights fade up on SCROOGE *in bed. He is snoring. All is peaceful.*

Church clock chimes twelve.

SCROOGE *suddenly wakes. He listens till it strikes twelve.*

SCROOGE What did he say? The first cometh at the last stroke of twelve?

(he looks around him. listens. calls out) Hello! Hellooo! Hah! Nothing! Twelve has struck and – nothing! It was all a dream! Three ghosts! Hah! There are no ghosts! Ha ha ha!

(calls again, bolder) O ghost!? Ghost!? Nothing. Nothing at all! Ha hah! I said gho-ost!

(calls louder) O ghosty ghosty ghosty!!!??? –

VOICE Mr Scrooge?

SCROOGE *freezes. He scrabbles for his candle, fumbles to light it, holds it out, peers into the darkness. A face appears behind him. Pale, immobile, unsmiling.* SCROOGE *turns. The face remains behind him. He turns back. The face is in front of him. The face is androgynous. Very quiet and still.* SCROOGE *shrieks.*

SCROOGE Who are you!!?

GHOST OF CHRISTMAS PAST I am the Ghost of Christmas Past.

SCROOGE Christmas what?

GHOST OF CHRISTMAS PAST Past.

SCROOGE Christmas past! What is that to me?

GHOST OF CHRISTMAS PAST 'Tis the key to thee sir.

SCROOGE I have all the keys I need thank you.

GHOST OF CHRISTMAS PAST Not all sir. Come sir.

SCROOGE Certainly not!

GHOST OF CHRISTMAS PAST But you called me, sir!

SCROOGE No I didn't!

GHOST OF CHRISTMAS PAST *(mimics) O ghosty ghosty ghosty!!!???*

The **GHOST** *snaps his hand on* **SCROOGE**'s *wrist.* **SCROOGE** *screams.*

MUSIC: DARKSEEKER DOGS - I AM LEGEND.

SCROOGE Ow! What are you doing!? Let go this moment!

GHOST OF CHRISTMAS PAST Tis time sir.

SCROOGE Time? Time to what?

GHOST OF CHRISTMAS PAST To journey to thy past sir.

SCROOGE Past!? There is nothing in my past! It's – it's past!

GHOST OF CHRISTMAS PAST Then there's nothing to be afraid of is there sir?

SCROOGE I am not afraid! Not a bit of it!

GHOST OF CHRISTMAS PAST Then why art thou trembling sir?

SCROOGE *(trembling)* I am not trembling. It is suddenly uncommonly cold suddenly as it happens and I am – I am – I am –

The back wall of the set lights up. **SCROOGE** *recoils, shielding his eyes from the dazzling light.*

Agggh! What is this – this LIGHT?

GHOST OF CHRISTMAS PAST Tis *thy* light Mr Scrooge.

SCROOGE My light! My light! I don't have a light!

GHOST OF CHRISTMAS PAST Oh yes you do sir. It has been darkened long enough. And now must shine as it should.

SCROOGE I have no wish to shine thank you!

GHOST OF CHRISTMAS PAST Come along sir.

The GHOST *pulls* SCROOGE. SCROOGE *shrieks.*

SCROOGE What are you doing! WAIT! I – I should warn you I am
in my night attire and cap which is hardly suited to exterior
pedestrian purposes! Not to mention a slight head cold which
I have in my – my head as it happens –

GHOST OF CHRISTMAS PAST There is much to be done sir.

She grabs his hand. SCROOGE *shrieks and leaves the
ground.* SCROOGE *starts to 'fly'. He shrieks again, eyes
tight shut.*

SCROOGE Heeeeelp!!!!!!

Music builds.

Lights flash.

Country Road – Christmas Eve

Birds in hedgerows, far-off church bell.

SCROOGE *and the* GHOST *stand together.* SCROOGE *opens his eyes. Looks about him. Blinks. Gasps.*

SCROOGE Where am I? Where is my house? My room? My bed? My bedposts? My bedsheets? What am I –

(gasps) But wait!

(peers around him) This place! I know it! It is –

GHOST OF CHRISTMAS PAST Where we begin sir. On Christmas Eve.

Approaching carriage.

The other actors play boys on a horse-drawn carriage. They charge across the stage whooping and cheering.

BOYS Merry Christmas! Merry Christmas! Happy holiday! Happy holiday!

SCROOGE I know these boys!

(calls to them) Pyckett, Hardstaff, Hetherington!

They appear to pass through him. SCROOGE *shrieks.*

They do not see me. Why did they not see me?

GHOST OF CHRISTMAS PAST They have no consciousness of us sir. They are but the shadow of things that have been.

SCROOGE I should have been on that carriage. It was going home for the holidays! Where was I?

GHOST OF CHRISTMAS PAST Where were you Scrooge? Remember?

Single tolling school bell.

Grimes Academy – School Room – Christmas Eve

MR. GRIMES *and* **MRS GRIMES** *enter. Black frock coat with cane. Desks are bought on.*

GRIMES Scrooge?

SCROOGE Mr. Grimes!

Enter **LITTLE SCROOGE** *(puppet, voiced by* **ACTOR 2***), aged eight. He is poring over an exercise book.*

GRIMES I said Scrooge!

LITTLE SCROOGE *(looks up, flinches)* Yes sir. Mr Grimes sir.

GRIMES I have heard from your father. He cannot take you home. So you must spend Christmas at the school. For yet another year.

LITTLE SCROOGE Yes sir.

GRIMES A burden and a toil for me and Mrs. Grimes – ain't it Mrs. Grimes?

MRS. GRIMES A burden and a toil indeed Mr. Grimes.

GRIMES But there we are. As ever sir expect no Christmas jollities from us sir.

LITTLE SCROOGE No sir.

GRIMES No fine plump turkey sir! Chestnut stuffing, roast potatoes, brussel sprouts or gravy sir! Gruel will be thy fare sir.

LITTLE SCROOGE Yes sir.

GRIMES Ain't that right Mrs Grimes?

MRS GRIMES Gru-el! Quite right Mr Grimes!

MRS. GRIMES *exits.*

MR GRIMES You have something to occupy you?

LITTLE SCROOGE My mathematics sir.

GRIMES Mathematics. Good.

> **GRIMES** *turns the pages with his cane. Spots a mistake. Whacks down with cane.*

> Compound interest boy! Compound! *Divide boy! Divide!*

LITTLE SCROOGE Yes sir.

GRIMES Stupid witless pointless child!

> *He lashes the page as he shouts.* **LITTLE SCROOGE** *flinches.* **OLD SCROOGE** *flinches too. The* **GHOST** *quietly watches the scene, watches* **SCROOGE** *watching.* **GRIMES** *spots something else. Another book beneath the exercise book.*

> What's this?

LITTLE SCROOGE *(tries to hide it)* Nothing sir.

> **GRIMES** *nudges aside the maths book with his cane. He reveals hidden beneath it an old leather-bound volume. It is a story book. He turns the pages. Each one reveals a picture.*

GRIMES Babes in the Wood!

> *(turns page)* Robinson Crusoe!

> *(turns page)* Sleeping Beauty!

> *(turns page)* Jack the Giant Killer!

> *(turns page) Ali Baba!! Open Sesame!??*

> **(GRIMES** *whacks the book)* A STORY BOOK!!!? Paltry pointless STORIES SIR!!?

> *(whacks again)* Where d'yer get this?

> **(LITTLE SCROOGE** *says nothing)* Speak up boy! Who gave it yer?

LITTLE SCROOGE Don't remember sir.

GRIMES Don't remember? Well we'll have a little look shall we?

> *He grabs the book. Picks it up.*

LITTLE SCROOGE No sir, please sir –

GRIMES *QUIET!*

> *(turns first page)* Ah yes. Here we are.

> *(reads)* "This book is for you my sweet darling boy. A book of treasures for your life. And if I cannot – "

LITTLE SCROOGE I beg sir, please sir!

> **GRIMES** *leers into the boy's face.*

GRIMES O my sweeeet! My darling boy! My little treasure! Aaaaaaah! Little wussy pussy diddums! Who wrote this GIBBERISH boy? Was it – mummy was it!? A little memento from mumsy-wumsy was it!!!?

LITTLE SCROOGE Don't remember sir.

GRIMES Don't remember? Don't remember? Well a fat lot of good she done you, din't she!? Pretty pictures! Little fairy stories! What use are they to anybody in the real world!? Mathematics is what yer need boy! FIGURES! FACTS! Exercises for the brain boy! Robinson Crusoe!? Ha ha ha ha!!! Babes in the Wood!? Sleeping Beauty!? Jack the Giant Killer!!? Ali Baba!!!? STORIES!!???

> *(he leers)* I'd write to little mumsy-wumsy if I were you and complain! Oh no you can't can you! Ha ha ha ha!!!

SCROOGE *(pulls away)* Need to go now please.

> **GHOST** *grasps* **SCROOGE**'s *wrist.*

GHOST OF CHRISTMAS PAST Not quite yet sir.

> **GRIMES** *looks straight into* **OLD SCROOGE**'s *face.*

GRIMES No use to you now is she boy?

> *He turns to* **LITTLE SCROOGE**. *Whacks the book on the desk.*

FILTH! Vile pointless FILTH!!! I'll give you Sleeping Beauty boy! I'll give you Ali Baba!

> *(whacks the book again)* I'll give you "Open Sesame" boy!

He lifts the story book high in the air so **LITTLE SCROOGE**
can see. Then slowly and deliberately tears it down the
spine into two pieces. He throws the pieces back on the desk.

NOW GET RID OF IT!! Lock it away! Out of the light of day
for ever!

LITTLE SCROOGE Yes sir.

GRIMES *(whack!)* Again.

LITTLE SCROOGE Yes sir!

GRIMES *(whack!)* Again.

LITTLE SCROOGE Yes sir!

GRIMES Good!

MRS GRIMES *(o.s.)* GRIMES!!!! Whatchoo doin' in there!?

GRIMES Coming my little petal. My little snowdrop. My little tiny
little –

(chuckling fawningly) – guinea piggy...

(to **LITTLE SCROOGE***)* Gerron on wi' yer work boy!

GRIMES *exits, chuckling and fawning.*

GHOST OF CHRISTMAS PAST Do you recall this book Mr. Scrooge?

SCROOGE *(says nothing)*

GHOST OF CHRISTMAS PAST It looked beautiful.

SCROOGE No memory of it.

GHOST OF CHRISTMAS PAST Not the sweetest of men, Mr Grimes.

SCROOGE It's what I deserved. Made me the man I am sir.

GHOST OF CHRISTMAS PAST Madam.

SCROOGE Whatever you are.

***MUSIC: ACTORS OFFSTAGE SING: THE COVENTRY
CAROL.***

CAROL SINGERS
LULLY, LULLAY, THOU LITTLE TINY CHILD,

BY, BY, LULLY, LULLAY.
LULLAY, THOU LITTLE TINY CHILD.
BY, BY, LULLY, LULLAY.

SCROOGE *(starts)* What's that?

GHOST OF CHRISTMAS PAST Just a Christmas carol sir.

SCROOGE Yes I'm well aware of that thank you! I'd like to go home now please.

GHOST OF CHRISTMAS PAST On our way sir.

SCROOGE Good! About time!

GHOST OF CHRISTMAS PAST To another home sir.

SCROOGE Another home? What other home? I have no other –

GHOST OF CHRISTMAS PAST Yes you do sir. Just eight years on sir.

SCROOGE Eight years – ?

> **GHOST** *takes* **SCROOGE** *by the hand.*

Wait! No! I have no wish to – take me back to my –

(to **CAROL SINGERS***)* SHUT UP!

The **SINGERS** *continue.*

Aggggghhhh!

SCROOGE *and the* **GHOST** *'fly'.*

Wait! Not again! What are you –

SCROOGE *howls as they go higher and higher.*

NO NO NO!!!

(staring down) HORRIBLE!! NOOOOO!!!

The company change the set below.

MUSIC: CORYNORHINUS – BATMAN BEGINS.

Scrooge's Boyhood Home – Christmas Eve

SCROOGE *floats down and 'lands'. The Ghost beside him.*
SCROOGE *panting with terror.*

YOUNG SCROOGE *(16) and* FRAN *(18) appear.* SCROOGE
freezes as he sees them. The GHOST *watches him.* FRAN
whoops.

FRAN Ebenezer! You're back!

FRAN *runs and hugs* YOUNG SCROOGE. *She kisses him.*

GHOST OF CHRISTMAS PAST Who is this? Scrooge?

SCROOGE No idea.

(pulling away) Need to go now.

GHOST OF CHRISTMAS PAST *(pulling him back)* Your sister. Isn't
it?

FRAN Oh I've missed you so!

SCROOGE Ow! What?

GHOST OF CHRISTMAS PAST Your sister. Fran. Isn't it?

SCROOGE Fran? Is it? Fran? No idea.

GHOST OF CHRISTMAS PAST Next part of your story Scrooge.

FRAN *(hugging him tight)* Oh Ebby Ebby! I'm so happy to see you!

GHOST OF CHRISTMAS PAST How she loved you!

SCROOGE Don't know what she's talking about! This is all pointless.
Not my story! I hardly knew her.

YOUNG SCROOGE How is father?

SCROOGE *starts.* GHOST *watches him.* FRAN *can't look at
her brother.*

He knows I'm here, doesn't he?

FRAN He won't come down. I'm so sorry.

YOUNG SCROOGE *(starts to go)* I'll leave then.

FRAN *(chases him, holds him)* No no! Stay Ebby stay! He won't always be like this!

YOUNG SCROOGE Of course he will! And why shouldn't he? Because I am no proper son. Because I am indolent and should be seeking employment. I should be looking now. This very moment!

FRAN It's Christmas Eve!

YOUNG SCROOGE So?

SCROOGE So?

FRAN He will not blame you forever Ebby.

YOUNG SCROOGE Well he should! He should blame me!

FRAN It was not your fault!

YOUNG SCROOGE It was my doing!

FRAN You were five months old!

YOUNG SCROOGE It was the having of me!

FRAN She was always sick. You just – weakened her.

YOUNG SCROOGE You see!

FRAN No no –

YOUNG SCROOGE That's why he hates me! That's why she –

FRAN *(grabs his hand)* Ebby!

SCROOGE We need to leave now please!

The **GHOST** *grips* **SCROOGE**'s *wrist.*

Owww!

FRAN *clings to* **YOUNG SCROOGE**.

FRAN No no! Ebby Ebby!

YOUNG SCROOGE Let me go!

SCROOGE Let me go!

Both **SCROOGE**s *pull away.*

YOUNG SCROOGE & SCROOGE LET ME GO! LET ME GO!!

FRAN *(suddenly)* Wait! Ebby! I could come with you! We could get away! Away from him!

> **SCROOGE** *freezes. Watches this moment.* **FRAN** *and* **YOUNG SCROOGE** *gaze at each other. They brighten with hope. Then sad again.*

> How can I? He watches me like a hawk. I am not even allowed into the garden anymore. He lives in perpetual terror he will lose me too. That I shall die like she did. And I fear it too Ebby. I am sick too. I know I am. If only I were stronger. I could come with you! I could! *I could!*

> *(she hugs him, holds him.)* O Ebby! Dearest dearest Ebby!

> *They both know this is impossible. Her closeness becomes unbearable. He breaks away.*

YOUNG SCROOGE This is pointless!

SCROOGE Entirely pointless!

FANNY I'm so sorry.

SCROOGE This scene you've inflicted upon me!

FANNY Don't hate me.

> **YOUNG SCROOGE** *looks at her, then turns and walks away.* **FRAN** *watches him leave.*

SCROOGE Pointless and irrelevant and entirely without purpose and – and – we need to LEAVE NOW PLEASE GHOST!

> **FRAN** *turns and disappears in the other direction.* **SCROOGE** *watches her leave.*

GHOST OF CHRISTMAS PAST What happened to her?

SCROOGE It was all a long time ago. I really don't –

GHOST OF CHRISTMAS PAST What happened Scrooge?

SCROOGE She married, had a son. Then she died. That's all I recall.

GHOST OF CHRISTMAS PAST Frederick.

SCROOGE Frederick yes.

GHOST OF CHRISTMAS PAST Your nephew Frederick.

SCROOGE Yes! My nephew Frederick! What about him?

GHOST OF CHRISTMAS PAST She died so young.

SCROOGE These things happen.

GHOST OF CHRISTMAS PAST You must miss her.

SCROOGE So do not seek to inveigle me sir with that which hath no –

GHOST OF CHRISTMAS PAST Both of you.

SCROOGE *(searches for his watch which is not there)* Time!!!! What's the time!!!? Cratchit!!? It's time Cratchit! Time to count the money! Cratchit!

> **SCROOGE** *runs round the stage.*

> Cratchit!!! Cratchit! The money Cratchit!! The box Cratchit! Unlock the box Cratchit! CRATCHIIIIIT!

GHOST OF CHRISTMAS PAST He cannot hear thee sir.

SCROOGE WHY!?

GHOST OF CHRISTMAS PAST He is beyond this realm sir. Come sir.

> *The* **GHOST** *guides* **SCROOGE** *away.*

> We need to journey a while longer sir, before we can unlock the box sir.

SCROOGE What!!? What journey? Journey where sir?

GHOST OF CHRISTMAS PAST Madam.

SCROOGE Madam!!

GHOST OF CHRISTMAS PAST To another Christmas Mr Scrooge. A merry Christmas sir.

SCROOGE Merry Christmas! Do You know nothing about me!!?

GHOST OF CHRISTMAS PAST I'm learning sir.

SCROOGE I detest Christmas!

GHOST OF CHRISTMAS PAST So we understand sir.

SCROOGE Good!!

GHOST OF CHRISTMAS PAST Still it must be undergone. If we are to find the grail sir.

SCROOGE The what?

GHOST OF CHRISTMAS PAST Grail sir. Holy Grail.

SCROOGE Holy –

> **GHOST** *grabs his hand.* **SCROOGE** *shrieks. They fly. They land.*

SCROOGE *(angrily)* That's the last time, the very last time you –

MUSIC: IRISH JIG.

The set dissolves and transforms into:

Fezziwigs Emporium – Christmas Eve

A large sign appears. **FEZZIWIG***'s abundant emporium – for all your family provisions.*

MR FEZZIWIG *appears. Rotund, jolly and Irish.*

Music builds.

FEZZIWIG *Wey-hey!*

Time for the Fezziwig Christmas party!

SCROOGE *Fezziwig? Fezziwig!?*

(gasps) I was apprenticed here! Old Fezziwig!

FEZZIWIG Time for dancing and feasting and games and dancing and more dancing! And more dancing still! Come my little Fezziwiggers! Never was there such a feast as the Fezziwig Christmas Eve! Wey-hey!!!

FEZZIWIG, ACTORS *and* **PUPPETEERS** *leap into the scene. They whoop, clap hands and change partners. The* **GHOST** *grabs* **SCROOGE** *and pulls him into the dance.* **SCROOGE** *resists but the ghost is too strong.*

SCROOGE No! No! Stop it please! Stop it!

SCROOGE *spins round with the dancers. They twirl excitedly round him. He sees them but they cannot see him.*

Music stops.

The **ACTORS** *skid to a stop.* **SCROOGE** *staggers dizzy and out of breath. He looks up and gasps. There in front of him is a girl. She is* **ISABELLA***. 17. Radiantly beautiful.*

FEZZIWIG Change your partners please!

Immediately the GHOST *bounces* SCROOGE *out of the way, while* FEZZIWIG *grabs* YOUNG SCROOGE *and puts him in* SCROOGE's *place.* YOUNG SCROOGE *sees* ISABELLA. *He freezes with panic. Tries to escape.*

SCROOGE Isabella!

YOUNG SCROOGE I'm so sorry – I really have to – I'm sorry – I – I – really must –

ISABELLA *holds out her hand. Laughing.*

– complete my – ledger – I'm sure someone else will be happy to – to –

FEZZIWIG Ebenezer Scrooge!!

SCROOGE Yes Mr Fezziwig?

YOUNG SCROOGE Yes Mr Fezziwig?

FEZZIWIG It's Christmas Eve my lad! Don't box yourself in boy! Don't be like young Marley who stays behind with his face of old parchment and his boxes and books and ledgers! There's a world out there don't you know! Stop all yer blessed counting boy!

YOUNG SCROOGE Yes Mr Fezziwig.

ISABELLA *waiting, smiling.*

FEZZIWIG Besides that's my own blessed treasure stood before you Ebenezer! And she don't look at just anyone you know! Why, the angels fall from heaven just for a peek at her so they do!

YOUNG SCROOGE Yes Mr Fezziwig.

FEZZIWIG So you goin' to dance with her or not boy?

YOUNG SCROOGE Would you – like to?

ISABELLA It would make me happy sir.

ISABELLA *stretches her hand.* YOUNG SCROOGE *tentatively takes it. She shows him how to hold her. He finds this very difficult.*

Music: builds.

YOUNG SCROOGE *and* ISABELLA *begin to dance. Slowly at first but gaining in confidence. She smiles as she guides him.* SCROOGE *watches them entranced. The* GHOST *watches him.*

Music: builds.

She whispers to him as they pass.

GHOST OF CHRISTMAS PAST Do I see your foot tapping sir?

SCROOGE By no means!

GHOST OF CHRISTMAS PAST My mistake. Sorry.

YOUNG SCROOGE *and* ISABELLA *spin round and round, increasingly enchanted with each other.* ISABELLA *tentatively kisses him.* YOUNG SCROOGE *tentatively kisses her back. They kiss some more.*

Music: builds.

YOUNG SCROOGE *takes a ring from his pocket. Nervously puts it on her finger. She smiles up at him. Kisses him.*

SCROOGE *watches transfixed.*

Music: fades.

FEZZIWIG *fades into the* SHADOWS.

YOUNG SCROOGE *and* ISABELLA *gaze into each other's eyes. They stay frozen as time stands still.*

SCROOGE A touching scene I'm sure spirit. But it served no purpose showing it to me.

(he claps his hands) Thank you! Thank you! That's enough thank you!

(they don't move) Why won't they move? Why won't they listen to me!?

GHOST OF CHRISTMAS PAST They are in the past sir. And the past is immoveable.

SCROOGE Well it's a relief it's over frankly.

GHOST OF CHRISTMAS PAST 'Tis not over sir. Two years on if you would sir.

SCROOGE Two years!?

GHOST OF CHRISTMAS PAST To another scene. Another Christmas Eve sir.

SCROOGE Another Christ – Spirit! Did I not just say –

The spirit waves her hands.

Crack of lightning and thunder.

YOUNG SCROOGE *has vanished.* **ISABELLA** *standing on her own.* **SCROOGE** *watches.*

Scrooge & Isabella's Home. Christmas Eve

YOUNG SCROOGE *marches on. He has grown grander. More stooped.*

YOUNG SCROOGE Isabella? What is it?

ISABELLA Ebenezer?

YOUNG SCROOGE What?

ISABELLA I have something for thee sir.

YOUNG SCROOGE What?

She holds out her hand. A flash of diamond.

SCROOGE Not this scene spirit. Not this Christmas!

GHOST OF CHRISTMAS PAST I am afraid it must be borne sir.

YOUNG SCROOGE Your ring.

She drops it in his hand. **OLD SCROOGE** *watches, frozen.*

ISABELLA It was my blessing sir. But now I return it.

(*closes his hand over the ring*) I fear you have another 'engagement' sir. That consumes your heart. Another passion sir.

YOUNG SCROOGE Passion? What passion?

ISABELLA All your gain sir! Your profits! Locking them up in your box every night of your life! That is your passion! Not *me* Ebenezer! I am not your passion! I am not your love! Where were you tonight?

YOUNG SCROOGE Working.

ISABELLA It is Christmas Eve!

YOUNG SCROOGE & OLD SCROOGE So!?

ISABELLA Tis the day we met! The day you proposed!

MUSIC: DISTANT CAROL SINGERS: GOD REST YOU MERRY GENTLEMEN.

YOUNG SCROOGE What time have I for Christmas! I have to work! I have my customers to see to! My books to be balanced! I do it for us Belle!

ISABELLA We were one beating heart Ebenezer. One. And full of joy. But now we are two and full of misery. How often and how keenly I have thought of this through the lonely hours of night I will not say to you. It is enough that I *have* thought of it and do think of it, and now – release you.

YOUNG SCROOGE Release me!? You cannot release me!

ISABELLA So leave your counting and your ledgers and your figures and your books and your MONEY! And come with me. For ever. With nothing! Just us!

YOUNG SCROOGE *stares at her. An agony of indecision.*

You cannot, can you?

Still **YOUNG SCROOGE** *says nothing.* **SCROOGE** *watches spellbound.*

Ebenezer?

Still nothing.

It is said if a man follows not the true calling of his soul, his soul will turn black and bad. It will wither and die. I hope you are following your soul's true calling Ebenezer. And that your soul doth thrive. May you be happy in the life you choose sir.

ISABELLA *turns and leaves. Both* **SCROOGE**s *watch her go.*

GHOST OF CHRISTMAS PAST You did not stop her sir.

SCROOGE For what purpose?

GHOST OF CHRISTMAS PAST You had her heart sir!

SCROOGE A distraction merely. A moment's weakness! A man must make his own way. He cannot afford such aberrations! She was a narrow escape if you want to know! That's all she was!

(he laughs) These – 'visions' do not touch me spirit!

GHOST OF CHRISTMAS PAST Just one more if you would sir. Then I am done sir.

SCROOGE I am done with thee spirit!

GHOST OF CHRISTMAS PAST Not quite sir. Ten years forward sir.

SCROOGE Ten – !!! NO!!!

Spirit waves her hands. Another mystic gesture. **YOUNG SCROOGE** *walks into a pool of light, older, more stooped, more like* **SCROOGE**, *head buried in a ledger.* **OLD SCROOGE** *stares at* **YOUNG SCROOGE**. *Their stance identical.*

MUSIC: CHILDREN SINGING 'AWAY IN A MANGER'

GHOST OF CHRISTMAS PAST If you would sir. *SIR!*

The **GHOST** *grabs* **SCROOGE***'s arm. She pulls him.*

SCROOGE Ow! OW!! Stop it!! Horrible, horrible flying, this is horrible. STUPID!

Pulls **SCROOGE** *into the next scene.*

Isabella's Home – Christmas Eve

Lights up on tableau. We see a woman sitting by a fire.

Music: singing continues.

SCROOGE Now where are we?

The woman stands suddenly. It is **ISABELLA**. *Ten years older. She looks straight at old* **SCROOGE** *and throws out her arms.*

ISABELLA Beloved!

OLD SCROOGE *gasps.* **GEORGE** *appears behind him. Laden with presents.*

GEORGE My darling!

SCROOGE *spins round.* **GEORGE** *runs to* **ISABELLA**. *He appears to run straight through* **SCROOGE**. *He runs into* **ISABELLA**'s *arms.*

ISABELLA Georgy! My darling darling!

They laugh. They hug. They kiss. The presents fall around them.

GEORGE Where are the children?

ISABELLA Listen.

SINGING: 'AWAY IN A MANGER' BUILDS.

GEORGE Happy Christmas Eve my darling. *(he kisses her.)*

ISABELLA The day you proposed.

GEORGE You remember?

ISABELLA Every day I remember.

GEORGE I was so nervous. I thought your heart might be elsewhere.

ISABELLA Never sir.

(she kisses him.) Never.

SCROOGE *gazes at the scene. The* **GHOST** *watches him.*

GEORGE Belle.

ISABELLA Yes?

GEORGE I saw an old friend of yours tonight.

ISABELLA Old friend?

GEORGE I passed his office in the city. In Fetter Lane. Quite by chance. His partner Mr Marley and he were counting their money. Heads bowed. Never once speaking. All the joys of Christmas Eve ringing in the streets around them. And they were sitting there. Oblivious. Like ghosts.

ISABELLA He would have killed me George. Sure as light is light. And snow is snow. If I had given him my heart. He surely would.

They take each others' hands. They kiss.

A narrow escape sir.

SCROOGE Cratchit!!! The box Cratchit!!! Cratchit!!!

He runs into the wings, runs back. Bumps into **ISABELLA** *and* **GEORGE**. *Sees they are still kissing. Shouts at them.*

Cratchit! I need – Cratchit!!! WHERE IS CRATCHIT!!

ISABELLA *and* **GEORGE** *are oblivious.*

GHOST OF CHRISTMAS PAST I have told thee sir. He is not here sir.

SCROOGE Yes! I know that! All right! Thank you!! I was just – just –

(gazing at them) That's all she wanted! My heart! That's what she kept saying!

(mimicking, dances round them) Your heart your heart! I hold you in my heart! Your heart is my blessing Ebenezer! Oooh yes it is Ebenezer! Your sweet tender heart Ebenezer!

ISABELLA *and* GEORGE *run out past* SCROOGE. *He shouts after them.*

BLESSING!!?? BLESSING!!?? A heart is not a blessing!!! A heart is but a muscle! An ugly beating muscle that keeps us going! Till we drop. That is all it is and nothing more and that's an end to it!

(laughs uproariously) Did you see HIM! Ha!!! Laden with gifts and Christmas humbug nonsense! Well he's welcome to her! And to think I might have married her! Hah! HAH!! Good riddance spirit! I thought you were going to show me some important scenes! From my past! That – that one could – well – learn from and – and – could educate one – and – profit from and – and – but frankly – they were – well frankly –

(he laughs) – a waste of time sir! A waste of precious time sir! Madam!!!!

GHOST OF CHRISTMAS PAST Precious time indeed sir.

The GHOST *vanishes.* SCROOGE *spins round.*

SCROOGE Spirit? Spirit!??

Looks for the GHOST. *Runs round stage, runs off.*

(o.s) SPIRIT!

Runs back. Shouts up to the flies.

You see! It hasn't worked has it!? I've defeated thee spirit! As I indicated to Mr Marley at his attempted 'haunting', thy journey has been wasted! Repent me of my life!? Ha! Well my life is mine own thank you! And I will do what I do with it and I will do it as I do it and THAT'S WHAT I'LL DO SPIRIT! So all your paltry pointless 'visions' are as dross! As chaff! As – as – bilge! I am unmoved! Undefeated! Unrepentant! Unchanged! Un – un – everything! Ha ha ha ha! *(he sings mockingly)* God Rest You Merry Gentlemen, let nothing you dismay, da da da da da da da da da da da da! O Tidings of Comfort and Joy, Comfort and Joy, O tidings of blah blah blah blah blah!!!

The **ACTORS** *appear behind him, singing, hooting, beating drums. They get louder and louder, more and more out of tune and raucous.*

MUSIC GROWS OVER THIS: 'EVIL COMETH'.

SCROOGE *holds his ears trying to drown out the sound.*

All music & sound cuts out.

Blackout.

End of Act One

ACT TWO

Scrooge's Bedroom – Christmas Morning

Lights fade up on SCROOGE *in bed. He is snoring. The candle flickering beside him.*

The church clock chimes.

SCROOGE *wakes with a start.*

The clock reaches the third chime.

SCROOGE *listens.*

SCROOGE Third chime! Third chime? What did he say?

(remembering) The second spirit on the third stroke of three expect!

He looks around him. Lifts his candle. Peers round the room.

There you see! Three strokes and – nothing! Not a second spirit in sight! All a nonsense! Hah!

(calls out) Ghost of Christmas Past!? Helloooo! Very frightening! Oooooo! Told the other spirits not to bother I wouldn't wonder! Quick you ghosts! Back home to ghostyland! Let's find some other dupe to haunt! Ha ha ha! Beat you second spirit! Before you even got here!

He disappears under the covers. We hear him chortling.

Back to ghostyland! Ha ha ha ha! Ho ho ho ho! Ha ha –

Stops chortling. Slowly turns over. Feels gingerly down the bed. Freezes. Peeks an eye out of the covers. Looks down. His feet appear to be rising up. He watches them with alarm.

Now there is a huge shape growing in the bed. He watches in increasing terror.

Agghhh! Agghhh!

He gingerly feels it. The shape grows. SCROOGE *shrieks louder.*

Agggghhhh!

The blanket flies off. A large jolly lady bursts out. THE GHOST OF CHRISTMAS PRESENT. *Covered in tinsel, baubles and bells. She wears an enormous dress.*

GHOST OF CHRISTMAS PRESENT *(broad cockney)* Hello darlin'!

SCROOGE *shrieks, leaps out of bed, runs round the room.*

SCROOGE Aaaagggh!

The GHOST *chases him, cackling with laughter. At the back of the set the* GHOST *swaps course so that when* SCROOGE *runs round to the front of the stage – they run straight into one another. Screaming.*

GHOST OF CHRISTMAS PRESENT Now where was we darlin'? Ah yes! Sorry I'm late dear. Still better late than never that's what I say! Gor blimey! You look a bit peaky! Ain't ya been sleepin'?

SCROOGE No if you want to know, I haven't slept a wink.

GHOST OF CHRISTMAS PRESENT Oh no! That's right. So you ain't darlin'! You must be EX-HAUSTED! Betcha could do with some lovely long bedrest – couldntcha darlin'?

SCROOGE Well yes actually I –

She pushes him on to the bed. Bounces on him.

GHOST OF CHRISTMAS PRESENT What was that darlin?

SCROOGE OW! OW! OW! OW! OW!

GHOST OF CHRISTMAS PRESENT Feelin' better now?

She cricks his shoulders.

SCROOGE Noooooo!

GHOST OF CHRISTMAS PRESENT That's good darlin'! So anyway where was we? Ah yes! So –

(Mrs Doubtfire Scottish) – what aboot all that then eh Mr Scrooooge!!?? All them 'Christmases Past' darlin'!? Spooky I'd say! Wouln't yer say?

She tweaks his nose.

SCROOGE Ow!!!!

GHOST OF CHRISTMAS PRESENT *(cockney again)* Still all long gone and forgotten now thank gawd! All them Christmases Past!

(wicked Witch of West. Peers at him) Or are they?

(witchy cackle) Anyway –

(cockney) – my turn now. Guess who I am darlin'?

SCROOGE I've absolutely no –

GHOST OF CHRISTMAS PRESENT The Spirit of Christmas *Present* dear! Of course!!!

She produces a sprig of mistletoe.

SCROOGE Aggghhh!

SCROOGE *makes a run for it. She gives chase again. On their second circuit the ghost re-enters with a butchers knife, Psycho-style.* **SCROOGE** *runs even faster.*

SCROOGE *Returns panting. Sits on the bed. Looks round. Thinks she's gone.*

That's better. Got rid of her! Hah!

GHOST OF CHRISTMAS PRESENT *jumps out of the bed behind* **SCROOGE.**

GHOST OF CHRISTMAS PRESENT Ta-da!

SCROOGE Arghhhhhh!

GHOST OF CHRISTMAS PRESENT Now then what happens is this see.

(pulls him to his feet) Ready darlin'?

SCROOGE No I am not madam! In fact I should like to make it quite clear –

GHOST OF CHRISTMAS PRESENT *(bronx accent)* Cut the gab nightcap man or you'll be sleepin' wid da fishies!

SCROOGE What!!?

GHOST OF CHRISTMAS PRESENT *(cockney)* You do what I say now darlin'!

SCROOGE Absolutely not! I most –

GHOST OF CHRISTMAS PRESENT *(mimicking earlier* **SCROOGE***)* Did you not hear me sir? I think thine ears are sealed sir!

She boxes his ears.

SCROOGE Ow!!!

She takes his hand. Becomes a Russian fortune-teller.

GHOST OF CHRISTMAS PRESENT O Scrooge, Scrooge, come with meee on a dark and dangerous journey to thine present Scrooge, so we can see how all them things thou didst in 'the then' has led to all them things thou doest in 'the now'. Or 'the present'. So to speak. Geddit?

SCROOGE What!!?

GHOST OF CHRISTMAS PRESENT *(cockney)* Course you do darlin'. Simple when you fink about it.

SCROOGE What –

GHOST OF CHRISTMAS PRESENT *(italian maestro)* SILENZIO!!

She produces a truncheon, stomps on his feet. Prods him in the stomach. And bops him on the head.

SCROOGE Ow!!!

GHOST OF CHRISTMAS PRESENT *(cockney)* Whilst all the while accompanyininin' me upon the blessed task for which I was born for darlin'! Just one day in the whole year dear. I only live this one special day then I am – guess what I am?

SCROOGE *(blank)* I've no idea...

GHOST OF CHRISTMAS PRESENT *(ghosty voice)* – no moooore!

(laughs) But while I'm 'ere dear I'm 'ale and 'earty dear! Visitin' the world! And spreadin' – spreadin'? Yes dear!? Come on! *Come on!!!*

SCROOGE Um – er –

GHOST OF CHRISTMAS PRESENT *(singing Ella Fitzgerald)* 'Have yourself a merry little Christmas.'

SCROOGE What!?

GHOST OF CHRISTMAS PRESENT Spreadin' Christmas cheer dear.

Tosses glitter over him.

SCROOGE What is *THAT!?*

GHOST OF CHRISTMAS PRESENT Christmas cheer dear. Get with the programme darlin'!

Throws glitter into his face.

SCROOGE *(splutters)* Yuk!!! Eurggh! Disgusting!!!!

GHOST OF CHRISTMAS PRESENT But it's Christmas dear!!!

SCROOGE *(spitting out the glitter)* Madam!!!

(sotto) You are a madam?

GHOST OF CHRISTMAS PRESENT Well I should 'ope so darlin'! Cheeky! *(slaps him)*

SCROOGE Ow!!! Perhaps – madam – I did not make myself crystal clear to your departed colleague – who I sent *packing* by the way! –

GHOST OF CHRISTMAS PRESENT What dear?

SCROOGE – that I – Ebenezer Scrooge – HATE CHRISTMAS! And any buffoon who –

GHOST OF CHRISTMAS PRESENT *(very fast)* – wastes his hours of righteous toil spreading Christmas cheer to all and sundry should be boiled with his own Christmas pudding and buried in his grave with a stake of Christmas holly through his heart! Ain't that how it goeth sir?

SCROOGE *(disconcerted)* Yes it is how it...goeth if you wish to – knoweth...yeth! And I am of that opinion still madam thank you! I do not see Christmas, I do not hear Christmas, I do not smell Christmas, I am oblivious to all Christmas!

GHOST OF CHRISTMAS PRESENT Where d'yer live then, in a cave?

SCROOGE Yes as a matter of fact, I do. I live in a cave of my own design and I'm very happy in it thank you. I know what you would have me spirit. You would have me *changed!* You would have me *repented*! You would have me – *converted!* But you will fail madam! I assure you of that! For I am –

GHOST OF CHRISTMAS PRESENT Gawd you're a talker! *(she whacks him with his pillow)*

SCROOGE Owww!!!

GHOST OF CHRISTMAS PRESENT *(recites, doggerel style)* Come fly with me upon this day, But a little time to pass dear. Come let me lead thee by the hand, Or by thy bony arse dear!

She kicks his butt. He lands on the stage.

SCROOGE Owww!

GHOST OF CHRISTMAS PRESENT Cos what day is it today darlin'?

SCROOGE I have absolutely no–

GHOST OF CHRISTMAS PRESENT CHRISTMAS DAY WHAT ELSE DARLIN'!

The **GHOST** *pulls him up and spins him round.*

MUSIC: FANFARE.

The **GHOST** *is waiting for him.*

Come along dear! Wheeeee!

They fly.

SCROOGE Agggghhh! No! No! Noooooo!!!!

MUSIC: LIEUTENANT KIJE: TROIKA. 0:26.

Over London Streets – Christmas Morning

GHOST and SCROOGE fly through the night.

GHOST OF CHRISTMAS PRESENT Oh look dear! The snowy rooftops of old London town.

SCROOGE *(eyes tight shut)* Agggghhh!

GHOST OF CHRISTMAS PRESENT Like a Christmas card ain't it darlin'?

(hoity toity) Get many cards this year dear? Hardly deluged I should imagine!

(laughs loudly) Ha ha ha ha! Ho ho ho ho!

(calls to the audience, tossing glitter) Merry Christmas! Merry Christmas everyone!

If the audience wave back, SCROOGE doesn't see. His eyes are firmly shut as he clings on. They bounce into an air pocket.

Whoops!

SCROOGE *(clinging on)* Spirit!!!

GHOST OF CHRISTMAS PRESENT Always a bit a turbulence over Kentish Town darlin'.

(gasps) But LOOK! Wait! Is it!? Yes! No! It IS! No! Is it?

SCROOGE can bear it no more. Peeks open one eye.

SCROOGE What!? What!??

GHOST OF CHRISTMAS PRESENT Is that not your nephew's house dear?

SCROOGE Nephew? Frederick? What?! Wait! Is it? No! Is it?

GHOST OF CHRISTMAS PRESENT The one with the lovely warm glow in the window dear. And the lovely twinklin' tree with all the presents under it. That one there dear.

SCROOGE gazes intrigued. He tries to see where she's looking.

No not that one there dear, this one 'ere dear. Ah! But then of course you would not know it darlin'. Never havin' been there. Then again you have no wish to go there do you darlin'? Invitin' you to Christmas once a year! A blessed nuisance if ever there was one, ain't it dear?

SCROOGE It's intolerable!

GHOST OF CHRISTMAS PRESENT Don't look at it dear.

SCROOGE I won't!

GHOST OF CHRISTMAS PRESENT Oh well all right then! Just this once! If you insist. Just a tiny glimpse. Seein' as it's Christmas!

SCROOGE What!? No! I said – NO! I don't want to go there! I don't – what!!? NO!

The spirit does her mystic gesture. **SCROOGE** *'lands' heavily.*

MUSIC: LIEUTENANT KIJE: BURIAL OF KIJE. 1:00.

Frederick's House – Christmas Day

A comfortable, warm and welcoming feel. Christmas tree, presents, baubles and tinsel. The sound of little bells.

Enter FREDERICK *and his wife* CONSTANCE. *They are laughing.*

CONSTANCE Your turn now.

FREDERICK My turn. *(thinks)*

GHOST OF CHRISTMAS PRESENT Who can that lovely lady be sir?

SCROOGE No idea.

GHOST OF CHRISTMAS PRESENT Course you do dear. That's Frederick's wife silly! Constance. *(she slaps him on the wrist)*

SCROOGE Ow!

GHOST OF CHRISTMAS PRESENT But then you've never met her of course have you dear? My mistake dear. Sorry dear.

FREDERICK Right. Got one.

CONSTANCE Is he...a man?

FREDERICK He is a man.

CONSTANCE A young man?

FREDERICK I wouldn't say a young man.

GHOST OF CHRISTMAS PRESENT What on earth can they be talking about darlin'?

SCROOGE They're playing a game.

GHOST OF CHRISTMAS PRESENT What? A Christmas parlour game dear? Sorry –

(mimics SCROOGE*)* – pathetic paltry Christmas parlour game dear?

SCROOGE Who Am I?

GHOST OF CHRISTMAS PRESENT *(looks at him)* Sorry dear?

SCROOGE The name of the game is Who Am I? Something like that. I forget now.

GHOST OF CHRISTMAS PRESENT Right.

CONSTANCE A nice man?

FREDERICK No. I wouldn't say – a nice man.

CONSTANCE A nasty man then?

FREDERICK You could say nasty.

CONSTANCE How nasty? Really nasty?

FREDERICK Really nasty!

CONSTANCE Really *really* nasty?

FREDERICK Really *really* nasty!

CONSTANCE The bogeyman?

FREDERICK Worse!

CONSTANCE Bluebeard!?

FREDERICK Worse!

CONSTANCE Beelzebub!!?

FREDERICK *(grins)*

CONSTANCE Worse than Beelzebub!!!?

FREDERICK Far worse!!!

CONSTANCE Who sir who!!!???

SCROOGE *Who sir who!!!???*

CONSTANCE I know!! Got it!!!

FREDERICK Who then?

SCROOGE *Who!!? Who!!?*

CONSTANCE *Uncle Scrooge of course!*

FREDERICK Uncle Scrooge! Uncle Scrooge!

SCROOGE Me?

FREDERICK *(monster acting)* Uncle Scroooge is coming to get you! Heh heh heh!!!! Scrooooge!! Scrooooge!! Scroooooooooge!!

Chases after her making wicked Scroogy noises. They run round laughing. He catches her. They kiss.

CONSTANCE Fred Fred!! You'll frighten the children!

SCROOGE Well I'm glad! Glad I frighten children! Children *should* be frightened! All children should be frightened!

GHOST OF CHRISTMAS PRESENT Thank you for that little pearl of parental wisdom dear. And whenever you're ready darlin'!

GHOST *pulls* **SCROOGE.**

SCROOGE No! What!? Wait! WAAAAIT!!

GHOST OF CHRISTMAS PRESENT Can't 'ang about darlin'!

They 'take off' again.

SCROOGE Aggghhh! Nooooo!

GHOST OF CHRISTMAS YET TO COME 'Cos now to other Christmases must we go. And not all so sweet as them was sadly. To the poor parts of London sir. You've heard of the poor parts?

SCROOGE I have heard of 'em. Little point in seeing 'em.

GHOST OF CHRISTMAS PRESENT Though you'd hardly think these ones poor, they done it up so nice. With so little sir.

SCROOGE Who? Who have?

GHOST OF CHRISTMAS PRESENT *(waves her hands. Mystic gesture.)* Behold sir if you would sir, please sir.

Cratchit's House – Christmas Day

ACTOR 4 *enters as* MRS. CRATCHIT, *humming* God Rest You Merry Gentlemen *as she sets up the* CRATCHIT *family table. The other* ACTORS *and* PUPPETEERS *play and voice the* CRATCHIT CHILDREN: KATIE, ABIGAIL, URSULA *and* PETER *using a variety of hats.*

SCROOGE *watches the ensuing scene. The* GHOST *watches too, sometimes standing beside him, sometimes not. She occasionally plays* MARTHA *the eldest* CRATCHIT.

MRS CRATCHIT *(calls off)* Katie! Abigail!

KATIE & ABIGAIL Yes mother.

MRS CRATCHIT Are you putting on your ribbons and your clean smocks?

KATIE & ABIGAIL *(VOICED BY ACTOR 5)* Yes mother.

MRS CRATCHIT *weaves in and out of* ACTORS *and* PUPPETEERS *as they assemble the* CRATCHIT *set.*

MRS CRATCHIT Peter – Lay this table be a dear.

PETER CRATCHIT Righto mother.

MRS CRATCHIT *(calls off)* Ursula?

URSULA Yes mother?

MRS CRATCHIT Gravy browning?

URSULA Tasty as anything mother.

MRS CRATCHIT *(calls off)* Martha – how's the turkey?

GHOST OF CHRISTMAS PRESENT *(as* MARTHA*)* Sizzling lovely mother.

SCROOGE *double-takes on the* GHOST *being* MARTHA.

MRS CRATCHIT Katie! Abigail! Are you ready?

KATIE & ABIGAIL Coming mother!

SCROOGE Who are these wretched people?

MRS CRATCHIT Oh heavens! Whatever's got Mr Cratchit then?

SCROOGE Cratchit!?

GHOST OF CHRISTMAS PRESENT That's right dear.

SCROOGE Cratchit's house!?

MRS CRATCHIT And Tiny Tim's with him. Little chap.

SCROOGE Tiny –

GHOST OF CHRISTMAS PRESENT Tim dear. He's the littlest.

SCROOGE Yes I knew that.

GHOST OF CHRISTMAS PRESENT Course you did dear.

MRS CRATCHIT Where *can* they be?

PETER CRATCHIT They'll be here in a jiff mother.

SCROOGE No odds to me what size he is.

GHOST OF CHRISTMAS PRESENT Quite sir.

> *(as* **MARTHA***)* Fret not mother!!

> **SCROOGE** *double-takes again.* **ACTOR 5** *runs in as* **KATIE**
> *&* **ABIGAIL.**

MRS CRATCHIT Katie! Abigail! There you are! Now help your
sister Martha!

KATIE & ABIGAIL Yes mother. Yes mother.

MARTHA CRATCHIT Come on girls less be havin yer!

KATIE & ABIGAIL Yes Martha. Yes Martha.

MRS CRATCHIT Everything ready Peter?

PETER CRATCHIT All ready mother.

MRS CRATCHIT Come along, come along!

ALL CHILDREN Yes mother!

MRS CRATCHIT *(looking through window)* Look Look children!
Here they come now! Father! And Tiny Tim!

ALL CHILDREN It's father, father! Father and Tiny Tim!

BOB CRATCHIT *enters with* TINY TIM *(puppet, voiced by* PUPPETEER 1*) on his shoulder.* TINY TIM *is a lame and sickly seven year old.* SCROOGE *starts when he sees him.*

CRATCHIT Happy Christmas my beloved ones!

MRS CRATCHIT Blessings be Mr Cratchit!

The GHOST *and the* CRATCHITs *cheer.*

And how did Tiny Tim fare?

CRATCHIT How did you fare Tiny Tim?

TINY TIM As good as gold as I hope mother! We went to the top of the hill and the snow was coming down. Big white flakes like feathers. And I looked right up, right into the snow and all the flakes were smiling. And I could see as high as Heaven!

He looks up. They all look with him. SCROOGE *looks up then destroys the moment.*

SCROOGE Just snow that's all. Just a meteorological fact!

MRS CRATCHIT *(wipes away a tear)* Good Tiny Tim, good!

TINY TIM And now I'm ready for my dinner.

Everyone cheers and claps. TINY TIM *claps too. He begins to walk.*

MUSIC: IN THE BLEAK MIDWINTER – KETIL BJORNSTAD – THE RAINBOW SESSIONS. 0:45.

He walks painfully but firmly towards the table. They all watch with baited breath. He sits painfully in his seat. Everyone reaches to help him.

I can do it! I can do it!

At last TINY TIM *sits. Audible relief as he does so.* SCROOGE *gazes wide-eyed. The* GHOST *watches him as he does so.*

GHOST OF CHRISTMAS PRESENT Tiny Tim dear.

SCROOGE So I gathered.

MRS CRATCHIT Ah my blessed boy!

(she kisses him) But –

(under her breath) – how was he?

CRATCHIT *(smiling bravely)* Strong and hearty as the best of 'em my dear Mrs C.

A painful moment. They know this isn't true. CRATCHIT *claps his hands.*

Now then my dearest ones! Where is our Christmas feast we heard so much about, eh Tiny Tim?

MRS CRATCHIT What did you hear father?

CRATCHIT What did we hear? Well that our turkey is a mighty feathered phenomenon. The greatest turkey ever known! That Ursula's gravy is hissing hot and Master Peter's potatoes mashed to a tee and Miss Kate and Miss Abigail's apple-sauce the sweetest this side of China and Miss Martha's chestnut stuffing fit for no less than our beloved queen herself!

MRS CRATCHIT exits. Returns with the turkey. It is tiny. Even SCROOGE *looks twice.*

MRS CRATCHIT Ta-da!

TINY TIM Ta-da!

CRATCHIT & CHILDREN Hooray!!!

She puts it on the table. MR CRATCHIT *carves.* MRS CRATCHIT *serves.*

MUSIC: THE HOLLY AND THE IVY - CELTIC TIDINGS - CHRIS CASWELL.

GHOST OF CHRISTMAS PRESENT Well darlin'? This is a 'profligate Christmas bean-feast' to be sure!

SCROOGE Profligate. Precisely.

GHOST OF CHRISTMAS PRESENT All 'humbug' ain't it sir?

SCROOGE Humbug! Exactly! Humbug!!

GHOST OF CHRISTMAS YET TO COME A sham and a fraud sir!

SCROOGE A sham and a fraud indeed spirit!

CRATCHIT But first a toast! To Mrs Cratchit and all my blessed Cratchits! Merry Christmas to us, my dears. And God bless us all!

TINY TIM God Bless us each and all and every one!

> *Everyone claps, except* **SCROOGE**. **CRATCHIT** *holds* **TINY TIM** *close, holds his hand in his.* **MRS CRATCHIT** *wipes away a tear. The* **CRATCHIT**s *tuck into their tiny turkey.* **SCROOGE** *gazes at the scene.*

SCROOGE This um – this – child?

GHOST OF CHRISTMAS PRESENT Tiny Tim darlin'?

SCROOGE Tiny – um – whatever, yes.

GHOST OF CHRISTMAS PAST What of him dear?

SCROOGE Will he – will they –

GHOST OF CHRISTMAS PRESENT – put him somewhere dear? 'Are there no workhouses'? 'No prisons' they could bung him in? Or up a chimney p'raps? Or down a coalmine? All on his own dear? In the dark dear? Children is highly prized in mines so I hear, 'cos the mines is so narrow and twisty-like. Or – better if he died. Do us all a favour. Wouldn't yer say darlin'?

SCROOGE So will he?

GHOST OF CHRISTMAS PRESENT What dear?

SCROOGE Die?

GHOST OF CHRISTMAS PRESENT I am the spirit of Christmas Present sir. I live but for a day. I cannot tell thee dear. Sorry.

SCROOGE Simply – simply I mean simply that if he should – er – die, it will grieve Cratchit presumably so it will make his work that much slower. Which will impact upon the exigencies and necessities of my business. Which is the reason I ask it obviously.

GHOST OF CHRISTMAS PRESENT But it would 'decrease the surplus population'? Would it not sir?

SCROOGE It would. Precisely.

GHOST OF CHRISTMAS PRESENT 'Boo hoo hoo but there we are'. Ain't that how it goes sir?

SCROOGE Indeed it is madam.

TINY TIM Tell us a story father?

CRATCHIT After supper Tiny Tim.

TINY TIM Will you tell us my favourite? Ali Baba and the Cave of Treasures.

SCROOGE *(starts)* Ali Baba?

TINY TIM When he finds the hidden treasure in the deep dark cave? Oh please father. When he says 'Open Sesame!'

SCROOGE Open Sesame?

GHOST *watches* **SCROOGE** *as the memory stirs.*

TINY TIM And finds the rubies and the diamonds and the bright blue sapphires? Oh please father please!

CRATCHIT *(hugs* **TINY TIM***)* I will tell it to us all little man, but first let us sing I do declare!

CRATCHIT, MRS CRATCHIT *and* **TINY TIM** *join in with* 'THE HOLLY AND THE IVY'.

SCROOGE *watches the family sing. Suddenly he can take it no more.*

SCROOGE Cratchit!! CRATCHIT!! Stop it! Stop it!! What are you thinking of man! SINGING!! And – and – frittering away money you do not even have on such pointless trivial Christmas – jollities!

The **CRATCHIT***s sing on, oblivious.*

CRATCHIT! The money Cratchit! Stop this! D'ye hear me! We need to count the money! Cratchit! UNLOCK THE BOX AND DO THE AUDIT CRATCHIT!

GHOST OF CHRISTMAS PRESENT He cannot hear thee sir. As we have been explainin' they are in another molecular dimension as it is known. *(einstein)* Or rather vill be known.

SCROOGE What!?

GHOST OF CHRISTMAS PRESENT *(cockney)* Don't ask darlin'! Now we must leave this vision sir.

> **GHOST** *waves her hands. The singing* **CRATCHITS** *fade.* **SCROOGE** *watches them disappear.*

SCROOGE Good! Good riddance to it spirit! Good riddance to all of you Cratchits!

> **GHOST** *waves her hands again.* **SCROOGE** *and the* **GHOST** *'fly'.* **SCROOGE** *shrieks again but getting used to it.*

Agggh!! Right. Now then if you'd kindly convey me to my home thank you, we can all –

Enormous crowd gathered. Sounds of men and women.

Now what!!!? What is that? That fiendish noise!!!?

GHOST OF CHRISTMAS PRESENT More wot you have not seen sir.

SCROOGE *(looks down. Strains his eyes to see).* What? What are all these –

(gasps as he looks down.) Where are we!?

Kennington Common, London – Christmas Day

GHOST OF CHRISTMAS PRESENT Kennington Common dear.

SCROOGE Kennington Common!?? Kennington!!??

(gasps again) There's thousands! Thousands and thousands of –

(nearly falls.) Agggh! Look at them all! WHO ARE THEY!?

GHOST OF CHRISTMAS PRESENT Just the homeless, that's all it is darlin'. Them as 'as nothin' sir. No work, no homes, just 'emselves sir. From all over Britain they've come. To seek the rights that is theirs sir.

SCROOGE *(shouts down at the crowd)* Layabouts! Criminals! Vagabonds! Who do they think they are?

GHOST OF CHRISTMAS PRESENT The People – is who they are dear. Not layabouts or criminals or vagabonds. Or wastrels as Parliament and the newspapers would have us believe. But orderly and sober and peaceable sir. Singin' at the city gates. Till they're heard darlin'.

SCROOGE *(covering his ears)* Well I can't hear them!

GHOST OF CHRISTMAS PRESENT *(pulls his hands from his ears)* LISTEN SIR!

SCROOGE OW!!!

ACTORS and **PUPPETEERS** *are the People of England. They sing.*

SONG: HARD TIMES OF OLD ENGLAND (TRAD)

ALL *(sings)*
OH PEOPLE OF ENGLAND I'LL SING YOU A SONG,
OUR HOMES ARE NO MORE AND THE WORK IS
   ALL GONE,
THE RICH HAVE IT ALL, THE POOR MAN HAS NONE.
AND IT'S –
OH, THE HARD TIMES OF OLD ENGLAND,
IN OLD ENGLAND VERY HARD TIMES.

SO TAKE TO THE ROAD, IT'S THE LIFE THAT
  WE CHOOSE,
WE MAY NOT HAVE SHELTER, NOT EVEN
HAVE SHOES, BUT WHEN YOU'VE GOT NOTHING,
YOU'VE NOTHING TO LOSE.

Huge crowd sing chorus, comes in with the actors:

(sing)
AND IT'S –
OH, THE HARD TIMES OF OLD ENGLAND,
IN OLD ENGLAND VERY HARD TIMES.
WE SAY OH, THE HARD TIMES OF
OLD ENGLAND,
IN OLD ENGLAND VERY HARD TIMES.

SCROOGE They should listen to the people governing, that's what the 'People' should do!

GHOST OF CHRISTMAS PRESENT I'd say their faith in the people governin' ie the Government is on the whole infinitesimal sir. Whilst their faith in the people bein' governed – i.e themselves – i.e the People sir – is on the whole illimitable sir.

SCROOGE 'The People'!? 'The People'!? This isn't about the people, this journey you've forced me on, this is about ME isn't it?

GHOST OF CHRISTMAS PRESENT Quite right darlin'! My mistake. Sorry! All about you darlin'. But –

(sees something) – well! That's a coincidence!

Sound cuts abruptly.

SCROOGE What?

GHOST OF CHRISTMAS PRESENT Cos 'ere *is* more about you sir, right 'ere sir. Wouldya credit it sir!?

Frederick's House – Christmas Day

FREDERICK's *house in place, exactly as it was.* FREDERICK *chasing* CONSTANCE *as they were before.*

FREDERICK *(monster acting)* Uncle Scroooge is coming to get you! Heh heh heh!!!! Scrooooge!! Scrooooge!! Scrooooooooge!!

Chases after her making wicked Scroogy noises. They run round laughing. He catches her. They kiss.

CONSTANCE Fred Fred!! You'll frighten the children!

SCROOGE No no no!!! We've done this bit! TURN IT OFF!! D'ye hear me!??

GHOST OF CHRISTMAS PRESENT Not all of it darlin'. Shh! Concentrate. Concentrate.

SCROOGE *and the* GHOST *watch* FREDERICK *and* CONSTANCE *as the scene continues.*

CONSTANCE You can keep your Uncle Scrooge! I have no patience with him.

SCROOGE Away with them spirit!

FREDERICK Well I am sorry for him.

CONSTANCE Sorry for him!??

SCROOGE *freezes. Listening intently.*

FREDERICK And I will invite him and I will keep inviting him.

CONSTANCE *(kisses him)* Perhaps you see your mother in him darling Freddy.

FREDERICK Perhaps I do. I may hate what he does, all the misery he brings, but – I cannot hate *him*. I should. I know I *should*. But I – cannot. And –

(remembers) – yes!

CONSTANCE What?

FREDERICK Something –

CONSTANCE What?

FREDERICK – well – shook him yesterday. When we spoke. We spoke of – love.

CONSTANCE Love? Scrooge spoke of love?

FREDERICK He railed at our marriage.

CONSTANCE Of course!

FREDERICK But there was something else.

MUSIC: SIXTH SENSE – MIND READING.

Something else there. I saw it.

CONSTANCE What?

FREDERICK For a moment only. In his face. A sudden haunting.

SCROOGE Enough Spirit!

GHOST OF CHRISTMAS PRESENT Quiet darlin' please!

FREDERICK Made me think. Love and the not getting of it –

SCROOGE SPIRIT!

FREDERICK – is bad enough. But love and the not *giving* of it can lock up a man's soul for eternity.

CONSTANCE kisses FREDERICK with the greatest tenderness. SCROOGE watches frozen, unspeaking.

MUSIC: TROIKA – LIEUTENANT KIJE 0:25 –

Happy jangling of door bells. Whoops and greetings, Merry Christmases, children laughing, boots stamped.

CONSTANCE and FREDERICK run off. SCROOGE watches as they vanish. He and the GHOST are left alone on the bare stage.

SCROOGE NO MADAM!!!!

Music and sound: cut.

We did not speak of love! Love was *not* spoken of! I do NOT speak of love madam! It is not a thing I speak of! Love! Love! Ha! I see your game madam! You make it all up! That's what you do! All this past and present nonsense! Just cheap MAGIC TRICKS! Mere chicanery madam! Skullduggery! That's all it is! To make me think I see what I do not! Well I am not a gawping gullible fool like Jacob Marley!

(mimics **MARLEY***)* Oooh! Ooooh! Repent! Repent! Change thine ways! Beg forgiveness old friend! No madam!! I am Ebenezer Scrooge! And repenting and relenting and CHANGING is not what Ebenezer Scrooge does! Beg forgiveness! LOVE! No madam! Scrooges don't beg forgiveness and –

The spirit listens calmly. **SCROOGE** *rants away.*

– Scrooges don't love! It is not in our natures to LOVE madam! Not in my nature! Not in my father's nature! Not in any of our natures! D'ye hear me ghost?!!? LOVE!!?? Love is HUMBUG!!!

GHOST OF CHRISTMAS PRESENT *(looking into his face)* What are these dear?

SCROOGE What?

GHOST OF CHRISTMAS PRESENT Tears darlin'?

SCROOGE TEARS!!??

(wipes them away furiously) Ridiculous!! Ha! Men do not have tears! Tears are aberrant to a man's nature. They are women's things. Because women cry. And women are not to be trusted.

GHOST OF CHRISTMAS PRESENT Why sir?

SCROOGE Because women LEAVE madam!!!!

GHOST OF CHRISTMAS PRESENT I am sorry for thee sir.

SCROOGE No I am sorry for thee spirit! You've had a wasted night. You and your colleague. *Colleagues!* You are done and I have won madam! Now if you'd kindly convey me back to my office.

Thank you. Tomorrow is my *counting day! My yearly audit!* When all sums are accounted for, all debts paid and all books balanced! I hope you don't charge for your ghosting by the way! If so you'd be making a massive LOSS! (*laughs uproariously*). In fact you'd better take out a LOAN! From YOURS TRULY! (*laughs uproariously again*)

Unbeknownst to SCROOGE, GHOST OF CHRISTMAS PRESENT *has exited.*

Ha ha ha ha! So spirit if you'd kindly –

He looks round for her.

– spirit?

The spirit is nowhere to be seen.

Spirit!?

He runs round the stage.

Spirit!

Shouts into the audience.

SPIRIT!!!

Lights change.

London street sounds. Horses hooves, barrel organ.

Scrooge's Counting House. Night

SCROOGE *staggers, spins around. Recognises his Counting House.*

SCROOGE Ah! Well. Thank you spirit! You finally got the point. I'm back! As I requested. Everything – Ah! Everything as it was. As we were! Splendid! My little Counting House!

(surprised) Surprisingly neat, but otherwise the same. Cratchit must have had a tidy up. Well done Cratchit! Everything tickety-boo! As it tickety should be!

(chuckles loudly) Don't expect a raise Cratchit!

(chuckles louder. The door approaches, **SCROOGE** *opens it to look outside)* No sign outside. Strange. Mmmm. Fog coming down.

(fog drifts in) Good old London fog. The world as it was. Me as I was. My money as it –

(freezes) My money!!!

He shoots off to get his money, reaching into his waistcoat pocket for the key. He freezes mid-stage. Realises he's not wearing his waistcoat.

Agggh! Nightwear! What am I doing in my nightwear? No key! Where's the key!? My key!!! KEY!!! CRATCHIT!!!!!

MUSIC: BARBASTELLA – 'BATMAN BEGINS' SOUNDTRACK.

The fog creeps through the door, across the stage, prowls into the Counting House.

The **GHOST OF CHRISTMAS YET TO COME** *silently opens the door and walks through it.*

SCROOGE *spins round. Sees the ghost. Gasps in terror.*

Agggggghh!!!

(calms down) Ah! First customer. Splendid. Charmed I'm sure. *Charmant charmant! Enchantee!* As the French would say. Or *parlez.*

(he laughs urbanely) Do sit down why don't you?

The GHOST *doesn't move.*

Very well stand if you wish. So – how may we assist? A little – loan perhaps?

The GHOST *doesn't move.*

Oh! A larger loan possibly? A VAST loan no less! Excellent suggestion!

(chortles merrily) Oh sorry!

(looks round for the phonograph) Where's the – er – normally we – er – Cratchit! Anyway – um –

(mimes winding it up. Mimics a tinny carol) 'We wish you a merry Christmas, we wish you a merry Christmas, we wish you a merry – um – ' Anyway – ha ha! Do beg pardon.

(proffers hand) Don't think we've been –

GHOST OF CHRISTMAS YET TO COME I am the third spirit. The Ghost of Christmas Yet To Come sir.

SCROOGE *(laughs)* Ah no no no no no! Clearly the message never reached you. I'm so sorry. I did tell her. You know, the last one. Her! I am beyond spirits. I have no further spiritual requirement thank you!

SCROOGE *chuckles away.* The GHOST *doesn't move.*

Thank you!

The GHOST *doesn't move.*

Besides it is not Christmas yet to come! It is *this* Christmas, the one we are *in* sir! Everything as it was, everything as it should be and everything as it – as it – jolly well will be! Hah! All I need is the KEY!

GHOST OF CHRISTMAS YET TO COME Key to what sir?

SCROOGE Key to what sir? Key to what sir? To my money sir! Idiot!

GHOST OF CHRISTMAS YET TO COME The money is gone sir.

SCROOGE freezes.

SCROOGE Sorry?

GHOST OF CHRISTMAS YET TO COME Gone sir.

SCROOGE Gone? *Gone!!!?* GONE!!!!!???

He charges off-stage. A terrible scream.

(off) AGGGGGHHHHH!!!!

He charges back. The **GHOST** *is waiting.*

Music: builds.

Where is it! My box!!! MY BOX!!! WHO'S TAKEN IT SPIRIT!!!??

GHOST OF CHRISTMAS YET TO COME The Queen sir.

SCROOGE The Queen? What she doing with it!?

GHOST OF CHRISTMAS YET TO COME Her Majesty's Treasury sir. They own it now.

SCROOGE Own it!? OWN IT!? That is not possible! Unless – Unless I was dead sir! Which self-evidently I'm not sir!

(he laughs uproariously) Ha ha ha ha ha!

(stops laughing) Wait! WAIT!

(truth dawns) I know what you're up to spirit. You have hidden my money to make me *think* I'm dead! And that I lie at this moment frozen, lifeless and alone in some dark, deep, dank, dolorous grave sir to make me – ha ha ha ha ha! – repent sir! Well, as I've said many many times sir, I won't be repenting sir! And I won't be CHANGING sir! Ha ha ha ha ha! So give me back my money Spirit of Christmas Yet To Come! D'ye hear me sir!!??

SCROOGE *dances about, shouting at the* GHOST.

I said d'you hear me sir!!!???

The GHOST*'s eyes start glowing. He grows in size.*

Oh no no no sir!! You won't frighten me sir! No no no! Just my money if you please sir!? My money!!!! And be quick about it! I COMMAND IT SIR!!! MY MONEY!!! MY MONEY!!! GIVE ME MY MONEY!!!

Music: cuts.

Keys at the door.

The door opens. CRATCHIT *enters.*

Ah Cratchit! At last! Thank God thank God! Just in time Cratchit!

CRATCHIT *walks straight past* SCROOGE.

Ah! You see spirit? He'll have hidden the box away for safe-keeping. That's what's happened. A slightly more likely explanation than yours I think spirit! So all is well. Ha! Cratchit? Cratchit?

CRATCHIT *looks at his key chain, chooses a key.*

Ha! The key! Ha! Look! He has the key! So Cratchit If you'd kindly show this – er – gentleman that my money's safe and all is well? Cratchit!

CRATCHIT *goes to a tiny single drawer. Unlocks it.*

No not in there Cratchit! My money's not in there! It wouldn't fit!

(laughs raucously) Ha ha ha ha!! What's the matter with you Cratchit? *Cratchit!!*

GHOST OF CHRISTMAS YET TO COME His mind is on other things sir.

CRATCHIT *opens the drawer.*

SCROOGE Other things? There are no other things! Where's the box Cratchit!

CRATCHIT *takes out something wrapped in brown paper.*

What are you doing Cratchit!!? What's this?

CRATCHIT *carefully unwraps the brown paper and there is the leather-bound story book from the school room. Faded and battered and still in two pieces but otherwise intact.* **CRATCHIT** *gazes at the book as the mist gathers around it.* **SCROOGE** *gasps.*

My book!

CRATCHIT *(looks up, calls to the flies)* Tiny Tim? If you can hear me where you are. Since your passing.

SCROOGE Passing? Tiny Tim?

CRATCHIT I would bring thee comfort my boy, wherever you dwell. I hope in a place of peace. But perhaps it is to seek peace for myself. For you are my light in the darkness little man. Please may I read to you as I used to? Only *I* knew where this was. He'd forgotten all about it. His book of treasures.

SCROOGE Treasures.

CRATCHIT I learnt the stories off by heart. I know 'em all now. Every one of 'em. Worth more than all the money ever made, Mr Scrooge sir. It is your heart you see sir. Even you had a heart would you believe Mr Scrooge?

SCROOGE *tries to reply but cannot. He watches spellbound.*

Even in two bits and all battered and locked away. But you kept it sir. Even though you didn't know you did sir. Even though you forgot it was even there sir. Some part of you, some tiny beating part of you, could not bear to lose it. And that makes all the difference. You kept it old Scrooge! Doesn't that bring hope to the whole rolling world sir? That a Scrooge can love stories?

That a Scrooge can have a heart? Even though he doesn't know it? Doesn't it, Tiny Tim? My dear one.

(he looks up) What shall we read?

(he turns the pages) I know. How about – your favourite?

SCROOGE *(whispers)* Ali Baba.

CRATCHIT Ali Baba. And the Cave of Treasures. And so I will Tiny Tim. But we always like reading this bit first don't we?

SCROOGE *stretches his hand and opens the book simultaneously with* CRATCHIT. *Very tenderly, they reveal the title page.*

(reads) "This book is for you my sweet darling boy. A book of treasures to guide your life. And if I – "

SCROOGE's MOTHER *appears from the* SHADOWS.

MOTHER – cannot remain with thee as the doctors tell me I must not, then know how very dearly I would do if I could, and how very nearly did I see this one Christmas with you – your first ever Christmas – that I know now I will not. How many many Christmases would I spend with you if I could. Just one more hour of life with you would be the dearest gift, no earthly riches could compare. But since I cannot, know that I will look over you and love you always as I always did from the first sweet breath you drew. And do so now and always will forever. With my eternal blessing. Your mother. Seventeen seventy-seven. Christmas.

SCROOGE *is overcome with emotion. Real tears fall. The* GHOST *watches.*

CRATCHIT So you was loved Mr Scrooge. All that time. Who'd a' thought it? Even though you never knew 'er sir. She loved you Mr Scrooge. And you loved her, didn't yer sir? Like all the Cratchits love Mrs Cratchit! Didn't you sir?

SCROOGE *(barely audible)* I did. I do.

Suddenly a voice shatters the moment. The GHOST *morphs into* GRIMES *the school master.*

GRIMES SCROOGE!!

SCROOGE *freezes.*

What's this!!? Robinson Crusoe! Jack the Giant Killer! ALI BABA!!? STORIES BOY!!? PALTRY POINTLESS STORIES!??

(raises his cane) Give me the book boy! Vile witless pointless boy! Give it to me!!! Scrooge!!! GIVE!!! SCROOGE!!!

SCROOGE Yes sir.

GRIMES That's right boy. Quickly boy quickly! I'm waitin' Scrooge! I'm waitin'!

SCROOGE *looks up at* **GRIMES.**

SCROOGE No sir.

GRIMES What!!? What was that!?? Whatcher say boy!? SCROOGE!!!!!!!?

SCROOGE I said no sir. It is my book sir. It is my most special treasure. Given to me by someone I loved. Yes, loved sir. And you're not to have it. Not ever. No-one is to have it. Except Tiny Tim. And Bob Cratchit actually. And all the Cratchits actually. And all the children of all the world actually if you want to know sir actually. *SO MR GRIMES SIR –*

(he takes a deep breath) GET THEE GONE SIR!

GRIMES *roars. He lifts his cane.* **SCROOGE** *does not flinch.* **GRIMES** *freezes mid-stroke. He tries to shout, tries to scream, but cannot.* **SCROOGE** *faces him, till* **GRIMES** *slowly inevitably dissolves.*

SCROOGE'S MOTHER *sings the* Coventry Carol.

SCROOGE'S MOTHER
LULLY, LULLAY THOU LITTLE TINY CHILD,
BY, BY, LULLY, LULLAY.
LULLAY, THOU LITTLE TINY CHILD.
BY, BY, LULLY, LULLAY.

SCROOGE *joins her softly. Their eyes meet. They sing the carol together.*

SCROOOGE & MOTHER
LULLAY TOO, HOW MAY WE DO
FOR TO PRESERVE THIS DAY
THIS POOR YOUNGLING
FOR WHOM WE DO SING
BY BY, LULLY, LULLAY.

The carol ends. **SCROOGE'S MOTHER** *fades.*

SCROOGE *alone with* **CRATCHIT.**

The **GHOST OF CHRISTMAS YET TO COME** *reappears.*

GHOST OF CHRISTMAS YET TO COME Sir?

SCROOGE Yes?

GHOST OF CHRISTMAS YET TO COME We must leave now sir.

SCROOGE Sorry?

GHOST OF CHRISTMAS YET TO COME Leave sir.

SCROOGE Leave?

GHOST OF CHRISTMAS YET TO COME 'Tis the end sir.

SCROOGE The end? End of what?

GHOST OF CHRISTMAS YET TO COME *becomes* **ACTOR 5.**

ACTOR 5 The play sir.

SCROOGE The play!? What play!?

CRATCHIT *becomes* **ACTOR 2.**

ACTOR 2 This play.

SCROOGE I'm not in a play!

Enter **ACTORS 3 & 4.**

ACTOR 3 Yes you are.

ACTOR 4 *(pointing at the theatre)* What do you think this is?

ACTOR 3 *(pointing at audience)* Who do you think they are?

SCROOGE Who?

ACTOR 5 Them.

> **SCROOGE** *sees the audience for the first time. Double-takes, staggers with shock.*

SCROOGE But – but –

ACTOR 4 But it's over now.

SCROOGE Over?

ACTOR 2 Because you're dead.

SCROOGE Sorry?

ACTOR 2 Dead sir.

SCROOGE Dead, don't be ridiculous I'm not dead. I can't be dead.

ACTOR 4 Dead as a doornail Scrooge!

SCROOGE Dead as a – no!! –

ACTOR 2 *(As **MARLEY**)* Can't get much deader than that Ebenezer.

SCROOGE NO!!!!!!

ACTOR 3 The faceless executioner comes to us all in his time, doth he not Mr Scrooge?

> The **ACTORS** *run excitedly around clearing the stage.* **SCROOGE** *chases after them, the words tumbling out as he frantically tries to stop them.*

SCROOGE No no no!!! I don't want to die! It's too soon! I'll – repent! I will! I'll honour Christmas in my heart and keep it all the year. I will. I promise. I'll be nice, I'll be kind I'll be good. I'll be –

> *(calls up into the skies)* Spirits! Help me! They'll help me – You watch,

> **ACTORS** *joining hands for the curtain call.*

ACTOR 2 We were the spirits.

ACTOR 3 *(as* **GHOST OF CHRISTMAS PRESENT***)* That was us darlin'! Ooooh Scrooooge!

ACTORS 2, 4, 5 Ooooh Scrooooge!

SCROOGE WAIT!! NO! NO! I beg of thee! I swear – I swear – I swear – I swear – I've – I've – I've – I've – CHANGED!!!

The **ACTORS** *stop. Look at* **SCROOGE**.

ACTOR 4 Changed?

SCROOGE *(he really means it)* Yes! Yes! Yes! Changed! Changed! I have! I have! I've changed! I've changed!

(falls to his knees) I have! I have! I really really really have! I have!

The **ACTORS** *look at each other. They consider. They decide.*

ACTOR 3 No, sorry.

MUSIC: HALLELUJAH CHORUS.

The **FOUR ACTORS** *grab* **SCROOGE***'s hands and march forward to take the curtain call. Bow and back. Bow and back.* **SCROOGE** *drags back but they pull him on.*

SCROOGE Wait! No! Stop! It's not the end! It's not! Not the end! I want to – I want to – I want to LIVE!

Wild audience applause over music. Whoops and cheers.

The **ACTORS** *run back, run forward again,* **SCROOGE** *forced to run back and forth with them.*

No no no!!! Let me live! Let me live!!! LET ME LIVE!!! I beg of thee! I beg of thee!!

He struggles with the actors. He tries to escape but they are too strong for him. He keeps howling but in vain.

I beg of thee! I beg of thee! I beg of thee! I beg of thee!

They overwhelm him. He vanishes from sight. 'I beg of thee' continues to echo round the theatre.

Blackout.

Music and applause climax and cut.

Lights fast fade up.

Scrooge's Bedroom, Christmas Day – Morning

SCROOGE *is wrestling with his bed-sheet. His bedroom magically reappeared.*

SCROOGE – thee! I beg of thee! I beg of thee! I beg of thee! I beg of –

Silence. His face appears. He grabs the sheet. Looks at it.

Wait! Thou art not a spirit! Thou art – a bedsheet!

(embraces the sheet) Dearest bedsheet! Lovely bedsheet! And look! My lovely bedposts!

(hugs the bedposts) Lovely lovely bedposts! How I love thee bedposts! And – ah!! My lovely window!

(lovingly stroking window) My lovely lovely window! With its lovely little Victorian windowcatch. And its lovely view of Dickensian London!

(opens window, shouts out) Hello there! Helloooo!

A **PASSER-BY** *enters.*

Look a lovely passer-by! Hello lovely Passer-by!

PASSER-BY *looks up, sees it is* **SCROOGE**. *Freezes with terror. Tries to run away.*

No wait! Dear sweet kind passer-by! Kindly tell me sir. What day is it pray?

PASSER-BY Why Mr Scr – Scrooge sir! What day sir? Why tis –

(flinching) – Christmas Day sir.

SCROOGE Christmas Day!

PASSER-BY Y – Y – Yes sir.

SCROOGE But what year sir?

PASSER-BY Y – Year sir? Four– fourteen eighty-two sir.

SCROOGE FOURTEEN EIGHTY-TWO!!?? Oh my God! I'm in Mediaeval England!

PASSER-BY Eighteen! Eighteen forty-two sir! Sorry sir. My mistake sir.

SCROOGE Christmas eighteen forty-two!???

PASSER-BY Christmas eighteen forty-two sir! Yes sir!!!

SCROOGE That's now isn't it? It's not the future?

PASSER-BY Certainly not the future no sir! Certainly now sir. Now as it ever was sir! Never could it be no more now than it is now sir!

SCROOGE Ah thank you thank you dear passerby sir! Dear sweet good perfect passer-by!

PASSER-BY Thank you Mr Scrooge sir!

SCROOGE I am alive!!!

(looks triumphantly up to the heavens) I AM ALIVE!!!

PASSER-BY ARGHHHHH!

> **PASSER-BY** *runs for it. Bumps into the* **BOY IN STREET**.

BOY IN STREET What's up?

PASSER-BY He's gone barmy!

> **PASSER-BY** *exits.* **SCROOGE** *whoops at the boy.*

SCROOGE I'm in a play you know!!!

> *The* **BOY** *looks at* **SCROOGE** *blankly.*

All about me!!!

(points to the audience) That's the audience!!!

(bows and waves to the audience) Hellooo!

(if they wave back) They like me! Look! They like me! Hellooo! *(engages individual people)* How are you? Are you? Really!!? How marvellous! I am too. Who'd have thought it, eh? Ha ha ha!

The **BOY** *is about to make a run for it.*

Dear boy, dear boy, wait wait I pray!

BOY *skids to a stop.*

Tell me dear boy, dear dear boy in the street?

BOY IN STREET Ye-ye-yessir?

SCROOGE Would you know – dear sweet child – whether, by any chance, they've sold the prize turkey in the fine poulterer's in Pudding Lane?

BOY IN THE STREET What the big white-feathered one as big as me sir?

SCROOGE What a delightful sweet exceptional boy! Yes yes yes the big white feathered one as big as thee child.

BOY IN STREET It's hanging there now sir!

SCROOGE Ah! Heaven be praised! Then speedily speedily speed thyself this very instant and purchase that enormous great white bird as big as thee and tell 'em to bring it here, so that I may pay 'em and give 'em the direction where to deliver it. Do it in five minutes, I'll give you a shilling. Do it in less, I'll give you five!

BOY IN STREET Five bob sir!!? Blimey O'Reilly!! Right this minute sir!

BOY *charges off.* **SCROOGE***'s bedroom disappears.* **SCROOGE** *slides across the stage.*

The Streets Of London. Christmas Day – Morning

SCROOGE Wheeeeeeee! I am as bright as a light and as light as a feather and as happy as an angel and as merry as a school-boy and as giddy and as dizzy as a drunken man.

(remembers the audience again, a florid bow) A Merry Christmas everybody! A Happy New Year to all the world!

(double takes) WHAT!!!!?? What did I just say!? Happy? Merry? Merry Christmas!!!?? I have never said Merry Christmas in all my life! All I ever said was hum – humbu – humbu –

(he tries to say humbug. Gasps) I can't say it! Hum – hum – hum – humber – no! No – hum – hum – hummingbird – humperdink – ha! Tis impossible to speak it!

(tries again) Humbu – humbu – humbu – Ha! Ha! Ha! What a wonder! Everything is a wonder! The world is a wonder! You are a wonder! I am a wonder! Christmas is a wonder! I love it! And –

(to audience) I love YOU! ALL of you!

(to individual person) And particularly *YOU* madam! I love you. I love YOU! D'you feel it too!? Isn't it – a miracle!!!

(sotto) Are you doing anything later?

(closer) For a little mulled wine and Christmas pud?

(loud) What am I saying? What's come over me!? Ah!!! I need to dance!

(does a ballet leap) I need to sing!

(snatch of bel canto) La la la la la!!! I need to – dare I say it? – skate! Let's SKATE!!

MUSIC: VOICES OF SPRING - JOHANN STRAUSS.

The other **ACTORS** *enter. They skate in formation towards* **SCROOGE** *as he pirouettes rather unsteadily, still in his nightcap and gown.*

Wheeeeeeeeee! I'm skating and I don't care!!!

They lead him round the stage in an elaborate skating routine. **SCROOGE** *is no expert, but what he loses in steadiness he makes up for in enthusiasm. Two skaters take him by the hands and swing him round, while the other two bring on a door with a Christmas wreath upon it. The first skaters deposit him at the door.*

Music: climaxes.

ACTOR 3 *becomes a* **HOUSEMAID**. *She sees* **SCROOGE** *and shrieks.*

Sorry.

HOUSEMAID Yes sir?

SCROOGE Wouldst thy master be at er –

HOUSEMAID Home sir?

SCROOGE At home yes.

HOUSEMAID Yes sir.

SCROOGE Thanks anyway. I'll just er –

He turns to go. Turns back.

On the other hand –

Leaves again.

No no –

HOUSEMAID Are you all right sir?

SCROOGE *turns back.*

SCROOGE Um – when you say – 'at home' – you mean –

HOUSEMAID At home sir.

SCROOGE Right.

She holds the door open. He plucks up the courage. Removes his top hat. Reveals the nightcap. Walks to the door.

Thank you my dear.

(walks in) Nice little hat by the way.

HOUSEMAID Thank you sir. Nice little hat yourself sir. *(curtsies)*

SCROOGE Thank you too madam. *(curtsies too)*

Frederick's Drawing Room – Christmas Day

FREDERICK *and* CONSTANCE *enter. They stop transfixed. The housemaid stands staring too.*

FREDERICK Bless my soul! Uncle –

SCROOGE – Scrooge. 'Tis I. Indeed. Forgive my –

(adjusts his nightcap) – slightly erm unorthodox attire. I had a somewhat – disturbed night you might say. Anyway I just wondered – um – if – well – how to put this?

(retreating) No no it is a bother. I can see. I am so sorry. Forgive me I –

CONSTANCE You are welcome sir.

SCROOGE Welcome?

CONSTANCE You are always welcome uncle.

SCROOGE Uncle? My – my dear Constance. I'm afraid we've never met. The blame lies with me. I have – I'm sorry to say – driven away those who might love me. I should explain – I – I -have been somewhat – haunted madam.

MUSIC: THE BELLS OF ADELAIDE – ST CUTHBERTS ('SPLICED SURPRISE MAJOR') CHIME ACROSS CITY.

CONSTANCE There is nothing to explain sir. You are our family sir. The haunting is done sir.

SCROOGE Family?

The PUPPETEERS *and other* ACTORS *appear with* FREDERICK *and* CONSTANCE*'s five children.*

FREDERICK These are our children by the way. All five of them.

SCROOGE Five! Goodness! Ah!! Hello. Hello. Hello. Hello.

(one hiding) Hello.

CHILDREN Hello. Hello. Hello. Hello. Hello.

SCROOGE Um – might I ask – just – um – one tiny small question – um – will – there be – um – will – we have um –

FREDERICK Christmas turkey uncle! Plum pudding uncle! Roast potatoes uncle! Chestnut stuffing and brussel sprouts and cranberry sauce and gravy and –

SCROOGE Oh my goodness! Oh my goodness! Cranberry sauce! *REAL GRAVY!* How splendid! How magnificent! How unutterably marvellous! Indeed! But – um – forgive me – but – er – will – will – will – there be – um – I cannot ask –

FREDERICK Ask uncle.

SCROOGE *(small voice)* – games?

FREDERICK Games uncle! Wonderful games! Wonderful merry games uncle!!

Music: bells build over:

Merry Christmas uncle.

SCROOGE Say that again please?

CONSTANCE Merry Christmas Uncle Ebenezer!

She hugs him. He freezes with ancient terror. She holds on.

FREDERICK & CONSTANCE Merry Christmas Uncle Ebenezer

> **FREDERICK** *hugs* **SCROOGE** *too.* **FREDERICK** *and* **CONSTANCE** *hold him together. The* **CHILDREN** *and housemaid join too. They all hug* **SCROOGE**. *Till* **SCROOGE** *slowly but surely melts. He hugs them back. They dance round laughing.*

SCROOGE Oh merry Christmas! Merry Christmas! Merry Christmas! Merry Christmas!

ALL Merry Christmas! Merry Christmas! Merry Christmas! Merry Christmas!

> **SCROOGE** *and the family exit, leaving the* **HOUSEMAID** *singing alone on stage.*

HOUSEMAID *(sings)*

    GOD BLESS THE RULER OF THIS HOUSE AND LONG ON
        MAY HE REIGN
    MANY HAPPY CHRISTMASES HE LIVE TO SEE AGAIN
    GOD BLESS OUR GENERATION WHO LIVE BOTH FAR AND
        NEAR
    AND WE WISH THEM A HAPPY, A HAPPY NEW YEAR
    OH WE WISH YOU A HAPPY, A HAPPY NEW YEAR.

Music: climaxes.

Lights – fast fade. Fast up.

Scrooge's Counting House – Boxing Day

SCROOGE *sits alone at his desk in his black top hat. He pulls up the collar of his big black coat.* SCROOGE *as we met him at the start of the play.*

CRATCHIT *enters. He creeps towards his desk.* SCROOGE *rises from the shadows.*

SCROOGE Cratchit!

CRATCHIT *freezes.*

I've had enough of this lateness Cratchit.

CRATCHIT Yes sir.

SCROOGE It's gone on long enough.

CRATCHIT Yes sir.

SCROOGE Too long. Too long. Far too long

CRATCHIT Yes sir.

SCROOGE And it's not to be endured.

CRATCHIT Right sir.

SCROOGE So I'll tell you what I'm going to do Cratchit.

CRATCHIT Yes sir?

SCROOGE I am going to –

CRATCHIT *waits for the axe to fall.*

CRATCHIT Yes sir?

SCROOGE – raise your salary Bob!

CRATCHIT *freezes.*

Twenty times! Thirty times Bob! Forty times! Fifty times! Oh Bob! Bob! Bob! My dear dear dearest Bob!

He rushes to hug him. **CRATCHIT** *shrieks, puts his fists up.*

CRATCHIT Keep away sir, please sir beggin' yer pardon sir!

SCROOGE *tries to hug him again.* **CRATCHIT** *crawls through his legs. Runs to the other side of stage.*

KEEP AWAY SIR KEEP AWAY SIR! Or I shall be forced to call for a straight-waistcoat and a big lady nurse from the Bedlam hospital sir!

SCROOGE Tell me dearest Bob. Did you receive a mysterious turkey yesterday?

CRATCHIT Turkey sir? We did sir!

(gasps) So it was – from *you* sir? Oh sir! It was bigger than Tiny Tim sir! Oh sorry sir, you may have forgotten sir, Tiny Tim is my little –

SCROOGE I remember Bob.

CRATCHIT You do sir?

SCROOGE And how is Tiny Tim Bob?

CRATCHIT With such fine good nourishment as that sir, we have every hope for him sir!

SCROOGE Thank the lord. Thank the lord indeed dearest Bob! And Bob?

CRATCHIT Yes sir?

SCROOGE My box of money. It is still here?

CRATCHIT Indeed it is sir.

CRATCHIT *and* **SCROOGE** *walk into the Deposit room where the box of money is. They repeat the same key routine as before. However the mood and music that underscore this routine is now lighter - things have changed.*

SCROOGE Now let us unlock it Bob and take its contents – that have enchained and enslaved me through my greed and selfishness even to the very point of death – and let me who hath, distribute all of it to all of them who hath not!

CRATCHIT Very good sir!

SCROOGE And we shall rid this world of the shackles of profit and greed! Of all owings and lendings and interests and borrowings and loans and penalties and bonuses and all other wretched devices that make one richer by making another poorer. I shall devote my life to it Bob. To make the world a good and kind and fair and happy place for all. And Bob?

CRATCHIT Yes sir?

SCROOGE I wonder – might I come to visit thy family Bob? And read to Tiny Tim? Read him – *Ali Baba?*

CRATCHIT Oh sir! *Ali Baba sir!* Yes sir! That would be a treasure sir, the greatest treasure ever sir. Or may I say – a blessing sir.

SCROOGE Blessing Bob?

> **SCROOGE** *clutches his heart. Starts to gasp.*

Bob! Bob!

CRATCHIT What is it sir!? What is it!?

SCROOGE My heart Bob!

> **CRATCHIT** *rushes to him, alarmed.*

CRATCHIT Your heart sir!? Your heart!!?

SCROOGE *(clutching his chest)* 'Tis – 'tis – 'tis – *(listens, laughs)* – beating Bob! 'Tis beating! Listen Bob! Canst hear it?

CRATCHIT *(leans in to listen)* Oh yes sir! I can sir!

SCROOGE But Bob Bob Bob!

CRATCHIT Yes sir? Yes sir? Yes sir?

SCROOGE Not only my heart dost thou hear. But every heart. Every heart in every part of all the world Bob. All beating together. As one great family. For that is what we are, is it not sir? A great family! Sharing the great journey of this life and the great blessing of this great rolling earth.

> All of us together sir! Are we not Mr Cratchit sir? Are we not sir?

CRATCHIT Oh yes Mr Scrooge sir, indeed we are sir! A great family! Journeying all together sir! Sharing the blessing of this great rolling earth and no mistake sir. Open Sesame sir! Open Sesame!

MUSIC: BRITTEN - NOYES FLUDDE: THE SPACIOUS FIRMAMENT ON HIGH. 0:00 - 0:27.

Epilogue

ACTOR 2 Indeed Ebenezer Scrooge was even better than his word. And he became as good a friend, as good a benefactor, as good an uncle and as good a man as good old England ever knew.

ACTOR 4 And from that day he had no further need for spirits, but lived upon the Total Abstinence Principal ever afterwards.

ACTOR 3 And past, present and future lived within him as one time. And as for Christmas –

ACTOR 5 – it was said of him ever after that he knew how to keep Christmas as well and true as any man alive.

ACTOR 2 As a time for giving and for blessing. And for love.

SCROOGE And so, as Tiny Tim observed –

TINY TIM *appears. He takes* **SCROOGE***'s hand.*

TINY TIM God Bless us each and all and every one!

MUSIC: HALLELUJAH CHORUS – MESSIAH: HANDEL

The company sing a medley of Christmas Carols. As they do so they act out bits of the play as if they were parlour games, blindman's bluff etc. **SCROOGE** *happily playing with them.*

The **ACTORS** *link hands with* **SCROOGE** *and take their true curtain call. Democratic at last, no master, no servants, all of them together, they sing with the audience:*

MUSIC: DING DONG MERRILY ON HIGH, GOD REST YE MERRY GENTLEMEN, WE WISH YOU A MERRY CHRISTMAS, HERE WE COME A'WASSAILING.

ENDS

Act One

Property list

Phonograph (p2)
Grandfather clock (p2)
Cord (4)
Garland – 'A prosperous Christmas Eve to all our Esteemed Customers' (p4)
Unwieldy ledger (p5)
Mrs Lack – throws snow over her head (p5)
Chair (p5)
Box of Victorian tissues (p6)
Deposit Room – full of drawers and boxes (p9)
Enormous chest (p9)
Large jangling chain of keys (p9)
Cratchit uses it to unlock another drawer which produces another key and so on – until the right key is revealed (p9)
A pound (p9)
Two pounds (p10)
Five pounds (p10)
Paper and quills (p12)
Mrs Lack – throws snow over her head (p13)
Frederick – throws snow over himself (p13)
Hat (p15)
Lavinia and Hermione Bentham - They throw snow over their heads (p19)
Cratchit, still clutching his book, takes their coats (p19)
Tissue (p19)
Loan papers and quill (p20)
Appointment diary and coats (p20)
Coins (p21)
Coats (p21)
Cratchit – throws snow after them (p21)
Hat (p22)
Frederick exits. Cratchit throws snow over him (p22)
Cratchit – throws snow over himself (p23)
Scrooge thrusts his hands into the coins (p24)
Single candle illuminating his face and in the other a meagre soup bowl (p27)
Candle (p35)
Desks (p40)
Exercise book (p40)

Another book beneath the exercise book...old leather bound volume. It is a story book. He turns the pages. Each one reveals a picture (p41)

A large sign appears. Fezziwig's abundant emporium – for all your family provisions (p52)

Young Scrooge takes a ring from his pocket (p54)

Costumes:

Four Actors – they are dressed in Victorian hats, coats and mufflers (p1)

Cratchit's hat, coat and scarf (p2)

Scrooge – Elegantly dressed in suit, cloak, bright waistcoat and top hat (p3)

Cratchit tentatively puts on his cap and muffler (p22)

Scrooge – nightshirt and nightcap (p27)

Mr Grimes – black frock coat with cane (p40)

Laden with presents (p59)

The actors appear behind him, singing, hooting, beating drums (p62)

Lighting list

A golden light shines out of the box (p9)

The golden light shines into his face (p24)

Lights come up (p27)

Lightning (p29)

Lightning (p29)

Blackout (p34)

Lights fade up on Scrooge in Bed (p35)

The back wall of the set lights up (p36)

Lights flash (p37)

Lightning (p55)

Lights up on a tableau (p59)

Blackout (p62)

Sound/Effects list

Door bell (p4)

The shop doorbell clangs (p13)

The shop doorbell clangs (p18)

Sound effects: Street sounds. Distant shrieks and cries of children (p24)

Sound effects: Loud London street sounds. Horses hooves, trundling coaches, barrel organ, people excited, selling wares (p26)

Sound effects and music stops (p26)

Sound effects: scraping chain sounds (p27)

Sound effects: chain sounds stop (p27)
Sound effects : chain sounds. Louder (p28)
Sound effects: chain sounds stop (p28)
Sound effects: chains (p28)
Sound effects: chains (p28)
Sound effects: whispering and laughing (p28)
Sound effects: flash of thunder and lightning (p29)
Sound effects: flash of thunder and lightning (29)
Sound effects: chains (p30)
A wild wind blows in (p31)
Sound effects: wind sounds (p31)
Sound effects: haunting sounds of grief and regret (p32)
Music and weeping build (p32)
Music climaxes – cuts out. Blackout (p34)
Sound effects: Church Clock chimes twelve (p35)
Music builds (p37)
Sound effects: Birds in hedgerows, far-off church bell (p38)
Sound effects: approaching carriage (p38)
Sound effects: Single tolling school bell (p39)

Thunder (p55)

Music/Carols:
CAROL: HERE WE COME A'WASSAILING (p1)
MUSIC (PHONOGRAPH): WE WISH YOU A MERRY CHRISTMAS (p5)
MUSIC (PHONOGRAPH): IT CAME UPON A MIDNIGHT CLEAR (p7)
MUSIC (PHONOGRAPH): WINDS DOWN (p8)
MUSIC: BARBASTELLA – 'BATMAN BEGINS' SOUNDTRACK (p9)
MUSIC (PHONOGRAPH): WE WISH YOU A MERRY CHRISTMAS (p15)
MUSIC (PHONOGRAPH): CUT (p15)
MUSIC (PHONOGRAPH): JOY TO THE WORLD (p19)
MUSIC (PHONOGRAPH): WINDS DOWN (p20)
MUSIC: SHOSTAKOVICH 8TH SYMPHONY-4TH MOVEMENT. 0-14 (P22)
MUSIC: FADES (P22)
MUSIC: SUICIDE GHOST – 'SIXTH SENSE' SOUNDTRACK (p24)
MUSIC: PROKOVIEV-LIEUTENANT KIJE: TROIKA (p25)
MUSIC: INTRO AND FIRST VERSE: CAROL – THIS IS THE TRUTH FROM ABOVE (VAUGHAN WILLIAMS-FANTASIA ON CHRISTMAS CAROLS) (p26)

MUSIC: SUICIDE GHOST – 'SIXTH SENSE' SOUNDTRACK (p29)
MUSIC: BATMAN BEGINS: VESPERTILIO (p32)
MUSIC: DARKSEEKER DOGS – I AM LEGEND (p36)
MUSIC: ACTORS OFFSTAGE SING: THE COVENTRY CAROL (p44)
MUSIC: CORYNORHINUS-BATMAN BEGINS (p45)
MUSIC: IRISH JIG (p51)
MUSIC: BUILDS (p52)
MUSIC: STOPS (p52)
MUSIC: BUILDS (p54)
MUSIC: BUILDS (p54)
MUSIC: BUILDS (p54)
MUSIC: FADES (p54)
MUSIC: DISTANT CAROL SINGERS: GOD REST YOU MERRY GENTLEMEN (p57)
MUSIC: CHILDREN SINGING 'AWAY IN A MANGER' (p58)
MUSIC: SINGING CONTINUES (p59)
SINGING: 'AWAY IN A MANAGER' BUILDS (p59)
MUSIC GROWS OVER THIS: 'EVIL COMETH' (p62)
All music and sounds cut out (p62)

Act Two

Property list

Sprig of mistletoe (p65)
The ghost re-enters with a butchers knife. Psycho style (p66)
She produces a truncheon (p67)
Tosses glitter over him (p67)
Throws glitter into his face (p68)
Tossing glitter (p70)
Christmas tree, presents, baubles and tinsel (p72)
Mrs Cratchit-returns with the turkey. It is tiny (79)
Cratchit looks at his key chain, chooses a key (p95)
Goes to a tiny single drawer, unlocks it (p96)
Cratchit takes out something wrapped in brown paper....carefully unwraps the brown paper and there is the leather-bound story book from the school room. Faded and battered and still in two pieces but otherwise intact (p96)
Christmas wreath (p108)
Box of money....same key routine as before (p114)

Costume:

The Ghost of Christmas Present – covered in tinsel and baubles and bells. She wears and enormous dress (p64)

A variety of hats (p76)

Scrooge – removes his top hat. Reveals the nightcap (p109)

Scrooge – black top hat. Big black coat (p113)

Lighting list

Lights fade up on Scrooge in bed (p63)

The candle flickering beside him (p63)

Lights change (p91)

The Ghost's eyes start glowing (p95)

Blackout (p103)

Lights fast fade up (p103)

Lights – fast fade. Fast up (p112)

Sound/Effects list

The church clock chimes (p63)

The clock reaches the third chime (p63)

The sound of little bells (p72)

Enormous crowd gathered. Sounds of men and women (p83)

Sound: Happy jangling of door bells. Whoops and greetings, Merry Christmases, children laughing, boots stamped. (p89)

London street sounds. Horses hooves, barrel organ (p91)

Fog creeps through the door, across the stage (p92)

Keys at the door (p95)

Wild audience applause over music. Whoops and cheers (p102)

Music/Carols:

MUSIC: FANFARE (p69)

MUSIC: KIEUTENANT KIJE: TROIKA. 0.26 (p69)

MUSIC: KIEUTENANT KIJE: BURIAL OF KIJE (p71)

MUSIC: IN THE BLEAK MIDWINTER – KETIL BJORNSTAD-THE RAINBOW SESSIONS. 0:45 (p79)

MUSIC: THE HOLLY AND THE IVY – CELTIC TIDINGS-CHRIS CASWELL (p80)

Cratchit, Mrs Cratchit and Tiny Tim join in with THE HOLLY AND THE IVY (p82)

SONG: HARD TIMES OF OLD ENGLAND (TRAD) (p84)

SOUND: CUTS ABRUPTLY (p85)

MUSIC: SIXTH SENSE-MIND READING (p88)

MUSIC: TROIKA-LIEUTENANT KIJE 0.25 (p88)

MUSIC: BARBASTELLA-'BATMAN BEGINS' SOUNDTRACK (p92)
MUSIC: BUILDS (p94)
MUSIC: CUTS (p95)
SCROOGE'S MOTHER sings the COVENTRY CAROL (p99)
MUSIC: HALLELUJAH CHORUS (p102)
Music and applause climax and cut (p103)
MUSIC: VOICES OF SPRING – JOHANN STRAUSS (p108)
MUSIC: CLIMAXES (p108)
MUSIC: THE BELLS OF ADELAIDE – ST CUTHBERTS ('SPLICED SURPRISE MAJOR') FADE UP IN DISTANCE (p110)
Music: bells build over (p111)
MUSIC: CLIMAXES (p112)
MUSIC: BRITTEN – NOYES FLUDDE: THE SPACIOUS FIRMAMENT ON HIGH. 0.00-0.27 (p116)
MUSIC: HALLELUJAH CHORUS – MESSIAH: HANDEL (p117)
The company sing a medley of Christmas Carols (p117)
MUSIC: DING DONG MERRILY ON HIGH, GOD REST YE MERRY GENTLEMEN, WE WISH YOU A MERRY CHRISTMAS, HERE WE COME A'WASSAILING (p117)

Milton Keynes UK
Ingram Content Group UK Ltd.
UKHW051053101023
R3430700001B/R34307PG429782UKX00001B/1